ESCAPE THE
TITANIC

ESCAPE THE
TITANIC

USE YOUR WITS AND SOLVE THE
PUZZLES
TO SURVIVE

JOEL AND JOHN JESSUP

IVY PRESS

Quarto

First published in 2024 by Ivy Press
an imprint of The Quarto Group.
One Triptych Place, London, SE1 9SH
United Kingdom
T (0)20 7700 6700
www.Quarto.com

A catalogue record for this book is available from
the British Library.

ISBN 978-0-71128-644-3

10 9 8 7 6 5 4 3 2 1

Puzzles and text by Joel and John Jessup
Design by Luke Griffin and Dave Jones
Editor Michael Brunström
Production Manager Eliza Walsh

10 9 8 7 6 5 4 3 2 1

Printed and bound by CPI Group (UK) Ltd,
Croydon, CRO 4YY

Contents

About this Book

This book comes from 'The Escapist's Library'. How did you come to have it? Perhaps it escaped. The books, like the escapist himself, can be rather elusive.

Each chapter herein offers part of a fast-paced adventure with four challenges.

The nature of each challenge will be revealed to you at the beginning, and everything you need to solve it will be shown on the pages. You may need to decode messages, find the meanings of symbols, and complete logical or numerical puzzles. There may be connections between puzzles you didn't anticipate, so check everything carefully. Clues and connections can be found anywhere in the text and images, and there are also hints as to how to reach the conclusion. Once you have solved the challenge you can move on to the next one.

If you need some help, there are some extra hints at the back of the book, organized by challenge. The solutions are also located there.

Good luck, and good escape!

Introduction

It is 11:40 p.m. on 14 April 1912 and the RMS *Titanic* is on its journey across the Atlantic Ocean, from Southampton to New York. According to the log, there are 2,224 people on board, passengers and crew.

Or is it 2,225? Because when the *Titanic* briefly stopped at Queenstown in Ireland, she took on an unexpected passenger: you.

You built her. Not single-handedly, of course, but you were a fitter at the Harland & Wolff shipyard in Belfast. As you helped build this incredible ship you were awed by her size and luxury, but even more by the possibility of a new life in America. But you couldn't get enough money. Even a third-class ticket costs more than you think you've earned in your entire life.

But you're smart. Too smart, many say. And you can lie well and think on your feet.

You waited until she docked in Ireland to collect cargo and passengers, removed the contents of a cargo crate and slipped inside. You can survive hiding in the hold for a few days, then sneak off when she arrives in New York!

Your plan was perfect. But like everyone else... *you never saw the iceberg coming.*

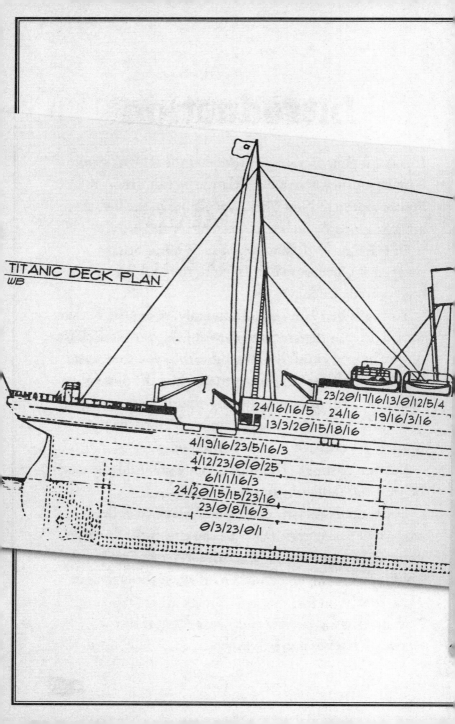

TITANIC DECK PLAN
WB

23/20/17/16/13/0/12/5/4
24/16/16/5   24/16   19/16/3/16
13/3/20/15/18/16
4/19/16/23/5/16/3
4/12/23/0/0/25
6/1/1/16/3
24/20/15/15/23/16
23/0/8/16/3
0/3/23/0/1

CHAPTER ONE

ORLOP DECK

—— 1 ——

Read the Deck Plan

You're woken suddenly by a freezing sensation... cold water is rising all around you. It's already knee-deep within the cargo hold. What's happening? The ship can't be sinking, surely? You've got to get out!

When you decided to stow away, one of the other shipbuilders – your friend William Bailey – gave you a hand-drawn picture of its decks but without the names included.

At the time you didn't know why he'd written numbers on it. You didn't even think you'd need to use it. But right now you feel that you can use all the help you can get, and maybe this plan could be of use if you can work out what the decks are called. Bailey also gave you a clipping from the *Belfast Telegraph* containing an interview with him. He said you'd find it helpful, but you couldn't see why.

TITANIC MAIDEN VOYAGE

The RMS 'Titanic' is to depart Southampton next week on its first official voyage.

The ship was built in the enormous Harland & Wolff shipyards here in Belfast, and many of this city's finest workmen and engineers had a hand in her creation.

One such individual, a master riveter named Mr. William Bailey, expressed regret that he would be unable to travel on the voyage himself, but waxed lyrically about the incredible ship's many extraordinary amenities, from its luxurious dining rooms on D Deck to the beautiful Boat Deck at the top, his favourite location. Mr. Bailey even said that if he had to give the 'Titanic's **A** Deck a rating between 1 and 10, it would be a **12**!

ORLOP DECK

You only realized later that he had slipped a small paper code wheel into your pocket too. To use it you need a code key, which is something that indicates one of the letter/number matches so you can line up the rest.

Where would you find that? Did William leave a clue?

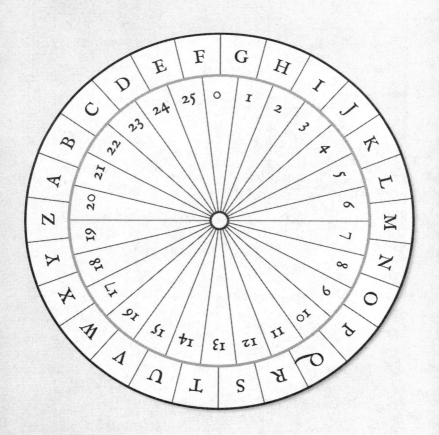

Once you decode the deck plan numbers you can put them here.

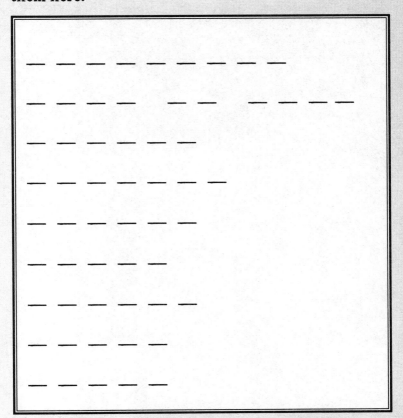

_ _ _ _ _ _ _ _

_ _ _ _ _ _ _ _ _ _

_ _ _ _ _ _

_ _ _ _ _ _

_ _ _ _ _

_ _ _ _ _

_ _ _ _ _

_ _ _ _

_ _ _ _

DECODE THE PLAN'S
MESSAGE TO FIND
THE USEFUL HINTS,
COMPLETE THIS
CHALLENGE AND
MOVE ONTO
CHALLENGE 2.

ESCAPE THE TITANIC

Escape the Cargo Hold

*William's extra message stuns you: is that true? Somehow
you have to find out. You rush to the door as quickly as you
can, but the rising water has caused one of the crates to fall
against the exit, meaning you are trapped!*

*Up until now the darkness and confined surroundings of
the cargo hold's many crates felt comforting and safe. Now,
with gallons of freezing seawater rushing in, it feels like it
could be your tomb.*

You grip the box and try to lift it up, but it's too heavy
for you. You've never managed to lift more than 15 kg
in your life. You can't even push it aside. Suddenly
you remember the cranes at the Harland & Wolff
docks: if you created a hoist system, you could use a
counterweight to lift the box out of the way.

You find some strong, if a bit wet, rope and, slinging
it over one of the overhead beams, tie it urgently to the
blocking crate. On the other end you secure a piece
of iron you find. You try using your weight to lift the
crate out of the way but there is nowhere to move it and
it drops back in front of the door before you can get
through. You need some other crates heavy enough to
act as a permanent counterweight...

You look at the other crates and realize their weights are marked on the sides, although some of the numbers have washed off. How can you tell which is which?

Once you know the weights you can work out what you need as counterweight for your system.

You suddenly see a manifest floating in the water, and realize it lists not just the crates in this stack, but also the crate by the door. If you can work out

Bertrand & Fils

Manifest

- **Wool** 5.0
- **Cotton Reels** 7.0
- **Flour** 7.3
- **Soap** 10.0
- **Canned soup** 10.5
- **Medical Supplies** 13.5
- **Champagne** 23.0
- **Nuts and Bolts** 30.5
- **Tools** 33.5
- **Hammer heads** 40.0

which crate is missing, you'll know how to counter-balance it.

WHAT IS THE WEIGHT OF THE CRATE BY THE DOOR? WORK OUT WHICH TWO CRATES WILL COUNTERBALANCE IT TO MOVE ON TO CHALLENGE 3.

Vent the Boilers

You lift the crate out of the way and quickly pull the door open. Underneath the crate, you find a flat cap (although maybe it wasn't flat before), and rush through the door, quickly closing it to contain the water... only to see that ahead of you every other compartment is flooding too. You have to get to the stairs and out of here!

In the cargo hold you got used to the heat and noise of the boiler rooms, filled with stokers piling coal in to keep the massive engines running, but now the air feels strangely cold, and it is filled with shouts of panic. The heart of the ship has stopped beating.

You enter the boiler rooms and make your way through them carefully, amazed by their incredible size. Everyone is too busy to notice you until you reach Boiler Room #4, and a crew member – with a desperate look in his eyes – grabs you. Are you discovered? You quickly pull the cap down low over your eyes.

'We've got to vent the boilers! They're going to explode if we don't send the built-up steam through the aft funnel. They've sealed the door until we get it done!'

He points to a series of valves.

'We've got to work out the right combination and send it to them on the Engine Order Telegraph. Once they're vented, they'll unlock the doors. But I've never done it before – none of us have!'

You've never vented a boiler before either, obviously. You've never stoked anything bigger than a bonfire.

Looking around, you find a manual showing the valves required to vent the boiler, and their order of activation. It also seems to have a confusing combination of letters and numbers in the bottom right corner...

1) AIR PUMP
FRAGILE AND PRONE TO BREAKING

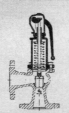

2) THROTTLE VALVE
THIS NEEDS MAXIMUM LEVERAGE TO OPERATE

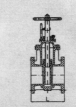

3) THRUST BLOCK
COMPLICATED DEVICE THAT NEEDS EXPERTISE

4) STOP VALVE
MUST BE TURNED AND HELD IN PLACE

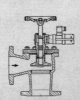

5) HIGH PRESSURE CYLINDER
VERY LOUD, CAN CAUSE EAR DAMAGE FROM HIGH PRESSURE

BOILER VALVES

TECAS	= 45
CATES	= 53
ETACS	= 12
CTESA	= 89

116

You also find the chief engineer's notebook with his personal insights about his men, presumably written for the head stoker. You frantically read it to see if it might help you work out who should operate which valve.

CHIEF ENGINEER JACK ELTHAM

Notes on stokers

Ernest – The most educated of the men, Ernest nonetheless is a little work-shy of the tougher tasks.

Callum – I fear Callum is overcareful with the machinery, treating it like it was made of bone china.

Simon – He has great strength but I must constantly instruct him when to finish a task or he will stay at it forever!

Thomas – This fellow's extreme height means that his very long arms are almost like levers.

Albert – The lad is completely deaf from a childhood illness and thus cannot be instructed by voice but is otherwise a very able-bodied stoker.

A picture of the men in happier times is pinned on the wall. The initials of their names remind you of some letters you saw recently...

Ernest

Callum

Simon

Thomas

Albert

Before you can even start though, you must work out which of the boiler pipes leads directly to the aft funnel.

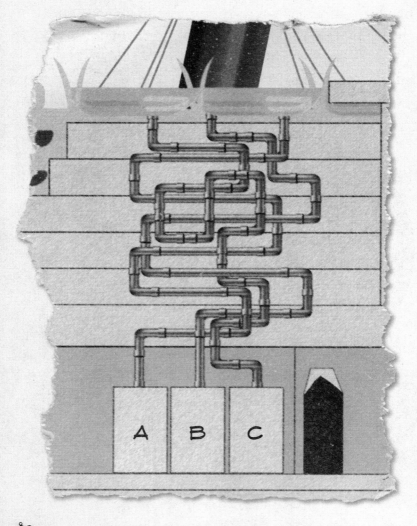

ESCAPE THE TITANIC

The device next to the boilers must be the Engine Order Telegraph that is used to communicate around the ship, but instead of the usual words there's a lot of letters and numbers. To what position should the handle be set? Perhaps those letters and numbers in the manual will help.

Until you get it right, the steam isn't going anywhere – and neither are you.

WORK OUT THE RIGHT TELEGRAPH SETTING TO VENT THE BOILERS AND MOVE ON TO CHALLENGE 4.

4

Follow the Rat

You feel the incredible surge of steam shaking the whole system as it fountains up through the aft funnel. The door is unlocked and the relieved stokers rush through it.

You separate from them to avoid scrutiny but get lost in a labyrinth of dark passageways.

Suddenly you hear a strange, shrieking, scrabbling noise, and then you are greeted by a horrifying sight: hundreds of rats running for their lives – and you've in their way.

Luckily, they seem more fixed on survival than attacking you, and you emerge unbitten by the panicking, furry creatures.

Bursting into the ship's electrical room, you see three of the rats making their way through the substations. Remembering what they say about rats leaving sinking ships, you wonder if following them might help you get to the stairs.

Above the substations you notice there are three strange plaques with Roman numerals and a series of letters and numbers written on them.

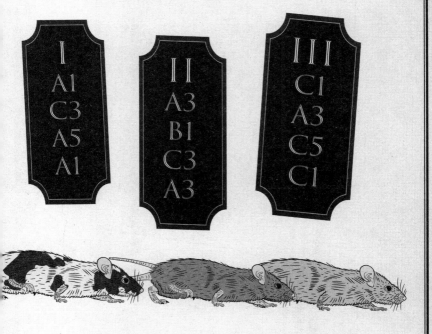

I	II	III
A1	A3	C1
C3	B1	A3
A5	C3	C5
A1	A3	C1

You notice Roman numerals marked on the floor plan in the junctions between the substations as well.

It seems that when the rats enter the junctions, they get hit by an electrical charge which makes them turn left, turn right or run forward depending on which Roman numeral is at the junction. How odd. In their frenzy the rats run the risk of getting caught in the various rat-traps that are laid around the room.

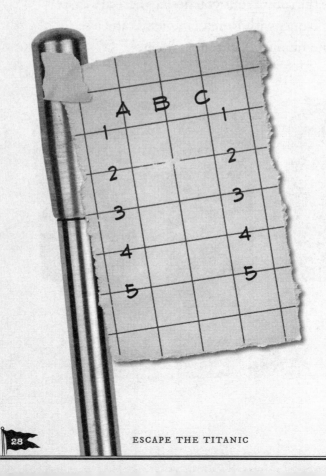

Pinned to a lever you find three pieces of paper with grids on them, but they don't seem to match the layout of the electrical room. You think it might relate to something else. ABC? 12345? You've seen them written somewhere...

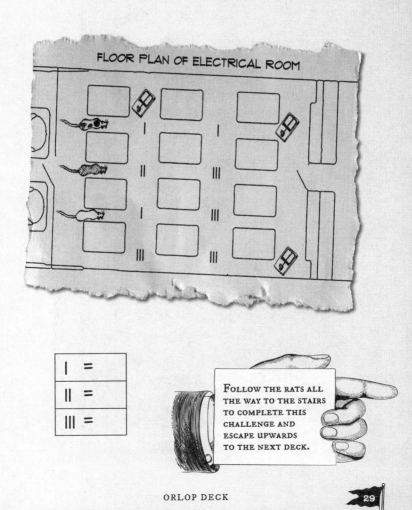

FLOOR PLAN OF ELECTRICAL ROOM

| I = |
| II = |
| III = |

FOLLOW THE RATS ALL THE WAY TO THE STAIRS TO COMPLETE THIS CHALLENGE AND ESCAPE UPWARDS TO THE NEXT DECK.

LEADING
FIREMEN'S
BUNKROOM

CHAPTER TWO

LOWER (G) DECK

— 5 —

Rescue Sharp

As you try to make your way from the Orlop Deck, you find the stairway up to G Deck crammed with third-class passengers and crew members. Looking for an alternative route you slip away from the crowds, down a rapidly flooding corridor. Suddenly you hear a faint call for help from a door labelled Leading Firemen's Bunkroom.

Opening the door to the room, you find it to be pitch-black inside. This time the voice calls louder: 'Someone please help – I'm trapped!' You consider leaving him but you can't abandon a man to a certain death. You cautiously feel your way into the dark room. 'I'm manacled to one of the bunks. Come quickly!' he shouts.

PLAN OF FIREMEN'S BUNK ROOM

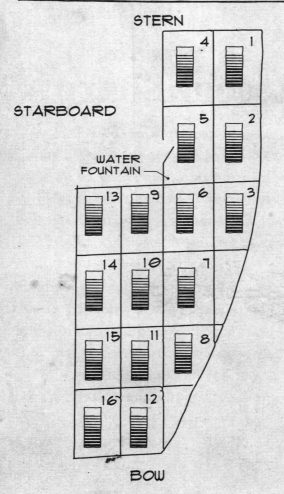

STERN

STARBOARD

PORT

WATER
FOUNTAIN

BOW

ESCAPE THE TITANIC

'Which one?' you ask. The acoustics of the room are too strange to allow you to follow his voice.

'I don't know the numbers... but I do have a route to come and find me. They blindfolded me and took me off the bunk to get a drink of water earlier. They led me on a highly circuitous route to try and disorient me, but I memorized the directions.

I got off the bunk at the stern/starboard corner,
turned to face the bow, and moved one bunk at a time
bow,
then starboard,
bow,
port,
bow,
port,
stern,
port,
stern,
starboard,
then stern.

ESCAPE THE TITANIC

Following the instructions, you rush up to the correct bunk, where the manacled man lies. Introducing himself simply as 'Sharp', he asks you to get the key for the manacles. There are five keys hanging in a box attached to a wall near his bunk but just out of his reach. 'Which one is it?' you say, fumbling for the box, while the water level rises around you. 'Its shape is the same as the path you just took!' he yells.

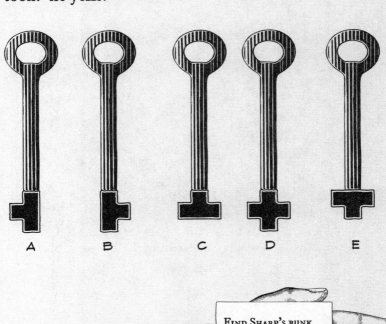

A   B   C   D   E

FIND SHARP'S BUNK AND THE CORRECT KEY TO OPEN THE MANACLES AND PROCEED TO CHALLENGE 6.

ESCAPE THE TITANIC

6

Find the Right Bag

You unlock Sharp's manacles and you both quickly exit the bunkroom into the now partially flooded corridor. 'I was visiting a girl in the third class, but her brothers caught me and chained me up in here. They just left me to drown,' says Sharp. 'Now let's get out of here – follow me, I know a shortcut to the next deck.'

You follow him through a door and into what appears to be a luggage compartment. 'Is this the shortcut?', you ask, confused.

'Listen, would you be a good chap and quickly find my brother's bag? Mama gave it to him. He'd be heartbroken if it goes down to Davy Jones' locker.' You think the situation's too urgent for this, but he's blocking the door so you relent. Oddly, Sharp doesn't know what the bag looks like. All he can do is show you a picture of his brother in a garden, tending to rare and beautiful plants.

Sharp also shows you a leaflet from the Chelsea Physic Garden, where his brother spends much of his time. It features illustrations of flora which he explains will also help to narrow down the right label to his brother's bag, especially if used with the picture of his brother. You think of remarking that he seems not to know a lot about his own brother, but with the freezing sea water gushing in, you decide that speed is the watchword.

Chelsea Physic Garden

Brief guide to plants and their properties

Witch hazel
(Hamamelis – medicinal)
Because of its astringent properties it is used to treat a variety of skin conditions.

Chamomile
(Matricaria chamomilla – medicinal)
Tea infusions can be made from the dried flowers and may improve sleep quality.

Rhododendron
(decorative shrub)
A large genus of roughly 1,024 species of woody plants, mostly native to East Asia.

Echinacea
(Echinacea purpurea – medicinal)
Frequently promoted for the prevention and the treatment of the common cold.

Venus flytrap
(Dionaea muscipula – exotic) A carnivorous plant native to the subtropical wetlands of the eastern United States.

Belladonna
(Atropa belladonna – medicinal)
Commonly known as deadly nightshade, the foliage and berries are highly toxic.

St John's wort
(Hypericum perforatum – medicinal)
A plant often used in the treatment of depression, menopause and anxiety.

'It's definitely one of these!' he says, indicating a group of eight seemingly identical bags. Each bag is tagged and on each tag is a single image. Which one is his brother's? They are a jumble of plant images and gardening symbols. You recognize a pair of secateurs, the traditional medical caduceus with two snakes, and an iron gardening trowel, as well as lots of different flowers. Which could have most in common with the brother?

FIND THE
CORRECT BAG
AND MOVE ON TO
CHALLENGE 7

ESCAPE THE TITANIC

7

Find the Right Pigeonhole

'Thanks, old chap,' says Sharp, politely, hefting the bag under his arm. He leads you confidently through a long series of corridors until you reach the door of the *Titanic*'s post room. 'Through here,' he says.

The post room is surprisingly large. Hundreds of thousands of letters were being transported to America, with postmen on board sorting them during the voyage. You're shocked to find that the *Titanic*'s postal staff, instead of trying to save themselves, are still hauling up mailbags from their storage area. The postmaster is instructing his staff to 'Save as much as you can!'

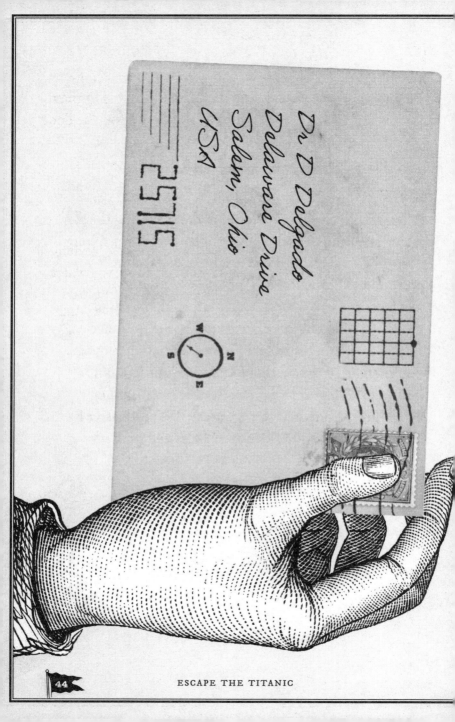

ESCAPE THE TITANIC

'You have to go. The water's coming up fast!' you shout, but they shake their heads. 'We have a duty,' they retort solemnly. Shrugging, you follow Sharp to the door at the end of the post room, but he finds it locked.

'Where's the key, man? Quickly!' hisses Sharp at a postman, who merely mumbles an apology then hands you a letter. 'I'm terribly sorry. In my panic I must have put the key where this letter is supposed to go.' He's pointing to the rows of pigeonholes. 'It's in one of them, I'm afraid.' He then starts telling you about his new idea for putting numbers on an envelope to help it get to its destination more easily. It sounds useful, but it's hardly the right time for a chat about sorting mail...

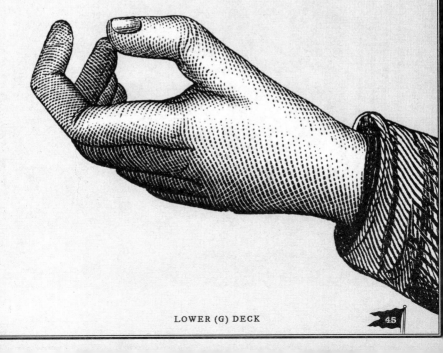

'Never mind that. How do we work out which pigeonhole it's in?' asks Sharp.

'All the information you need to follow a path to the right hole are contained on the front of the envelope. It shows you where to start, what your path is, and the direction of your pigeonhole,' replies the postmaster. He then leaves you with the letter and rushes back to his task.

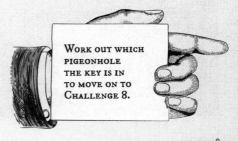

WORK OUT WHICH
PIGEONHOLE
THE KEY IS IN
TO MOVE ON TO
CHALLENGE 8.

ESCAPE THE TITANIC

8

Get through the Gate

Sharp is ahead of you, wading through the numbingly cold water towards an elaborate gate at the end of the corridor.

'Here we are. This should get us to the upper decks,' he cackles. Gripping his brother's bag in one hand, he does something to the gate which you can't see because he's blocking your view. It swings open. Sharp passes through but as you try to follow him he slams it shut from the other side.

'Terribly sorry, but this stairwell isn't for filthy stowaways!' he says, his voice cruel and mocking. 'Say hello to Davy Jones!' He runs up the stairs laughing, leaving you to rattle the gate furiously as the water reaches your chest. Putting your anger aside, there must be some trick to opening it...

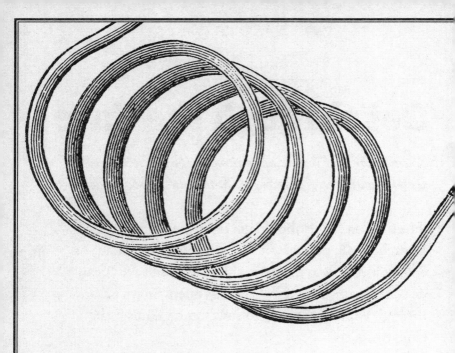

You're sure he pressed something on the gate, is there some kind of hidden device? But where? Some of the panels are now submerged, so in order to see them you will have to duck your head under water and hold your breath. Luckily there is a fractured air pipe spewing bubbles into the water. Can you get enough air into your lungs to stay under long enough to examine the panels? Starting from the top left, move from bubble to bubble collecting seconds of air. You will need two minutes (120 seconds) to work out how to open the gates. You cannot visit a bubble more than once.

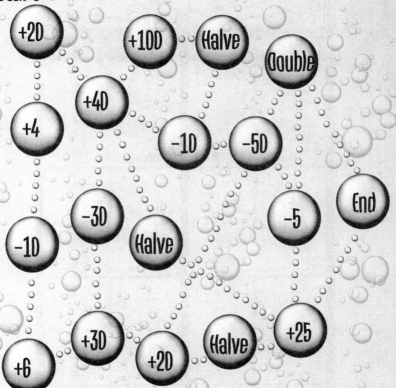

Start

+20

+100 Halve Double

+40

+4

-10 -50

-30 Halve

-5 End

-10

+6 +30 +20 Halve +25

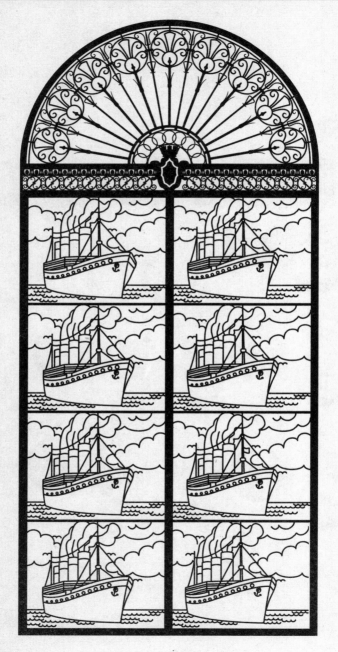

ESCAPE THE TITANIC

The number of seconds of air you gathered from the bubbles is now your time limit to solve this puzzle. The gate was designed for the first-class deck but was clearly put down here in third class for some reason. Six of the panels contain small, almost imperceptible, anomalies. It seems that all you have to do to release the lock and get through is to press the two panels that are identical, simultaneously. The water is up to your shoulders now and you can feel your arms and legs going numb... You must act quickly.

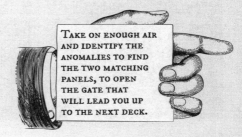

TAKE ON ENOUGH AIR AND IDENTIFY THE ANOMALIES TO FIND THE TWO MATCHING PANELS, TO OPEN THE GATE THAT WILL LEAD YOU UP TO THE NEXT DECK.

TITANIC

F

DECK

ESCAPE THE TITANIC

CHAPTER THREE

MIDDLE (F) DECK

—— 9 ——

Find the Right Door

As you rush up the stairs from G Deck Titanic groans and lurches sideways. The freezing water is already sloshing around your ankles, rising almost as fast as you can run. Panting, you find yourself on the Middle Deck, or as a nearby plaque suggests, F Deck. Around you people are rushing in every direction, and there are no clear instructions from the few crew that are present. You realize that somehow you must find your way up and out.

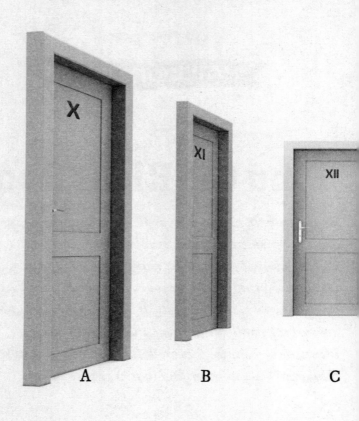

X   XI   XII

A   B   C

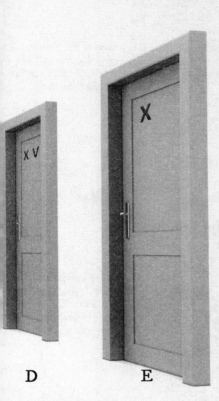

D   E

Ahead of you in the corridor are five doors, marked with wooden Roman numerals. But the number order doesn't seem right. Why are they like that? Why are there small pieces of wood floating around in the water? Once you know what the correct markings are, you wonder which of these doors could lead you to safety.

There are also five passengers here, panicking and shouting. You ask each of them if they know which door is the right way out, but you are bombarded by a flurry of different statements...

ESCAPE THE TITANIC

You recognize some of these people from when you snuck on board, and the identity of others is obvious from their attire:

1. Callum Blackstaff, bank manager
2. Robert Cloutier, baker
3. Helen Poole, governess
4. Able seaman Donald Palmer, crew member
5. Francis McGillvray, journalist

By listening to their answers, it's clear that only two of them are telling you the truth. But without knowing them personally, you must just try to think logically about who can or cannot be lying. However, of those two, surely only one of them must know the fastest possible route. It must be something to do with those incorrectly numbered doors.

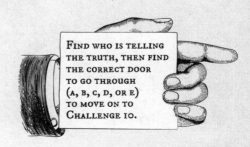

FIND WHO IS TELLING THE TRUTH, THEN FIND THE CORRECT DOOR TO GO THROUGH (A, B, C, D, OR E) TO MOVE ON TO CHALLENGE 10.

ESCAPE THE TITANIC

10

Save the Drowning Man

You stagger through what you believe is the right door only to find yourself not in a safe place, but in Titanic*'s swimming pool. A man seems to have fallen in and is thrashing about, apparently unable to swim.*

It's not in your nature to leave someone in obvious distress, but there is one major obstacle: you can't swim either. You spot a life ring but you'll need a way to haul him out. The electrical cable that powered the lights has fallen from the ceiling – that might work as a rope. However, it's still electrified. A nearby switch would turn it off, but the faulty switch is electrified too.

You decide you could use a nearby rubber quoit to pull at the switch, then tie the safely non-electrified cable to the life ring. You spot a towel on the side you can wrap him in once you have rescued him.

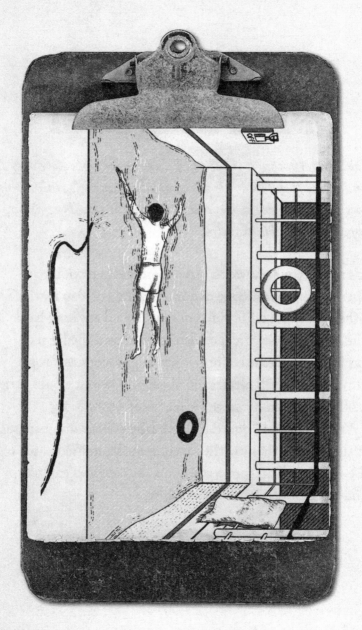

ESCAPE THE TITANIC

On the image opposite, draw three lines:

One to connect the quoit to the switch.
One to connect the life ring to the cable.
One to connect the towel to the drowning man.

The lines must not cross each other or go outside the frame of the picture.

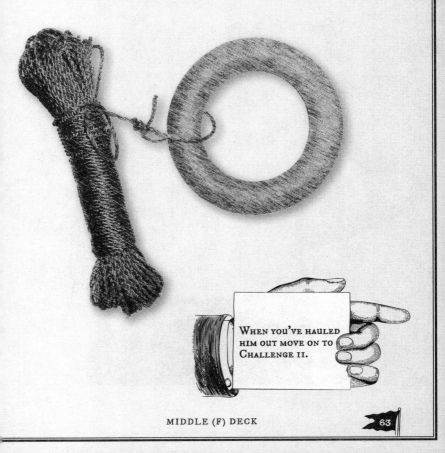

WHEN YOU'VE HAULED HIM OUT MOVE ON TO CHALLENGE 11.

ESCAPE THE TITANIC

11

Interpret the Tattoos

The man you've saved from the pool is covered in tattoos. He must be a sailor. Or is he? It looks like he's trying to tell you something but he is incoherent after his ordeal.

He starts pointing to the illustrations that adorn his torso. They seem confusing, but you can deduce a few things about the man straight away. During his semi-coherent babbling it becomes clear that he is trying to tell you where his cabin is, as there seems to be some kind of escape method there. His tattoos will allow you to work out which cabin is his with the further help of a nearby second-class cabin plan on the wall...

a. Three unicorns
What does this mean?
A. His surname is Tripplehorn
B. He likes odd numbers
C. He seeks purity

b. Two sinking ships
What does this mean?
A. He's been on two ships that have sunk
B. He believes in sea monsters
C. He dislikes even numbers

c. A skeleton that is being sick
What does this mean?
A. He gets seasick whenever he can see the sea?
B. He's afraid of vomiting skeletons
C. He just liked the picture

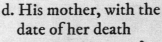

d. His mother, with the date of her death

What does this mean?

A. He avoids the number 9.

B. He has a large hat in his cabin

C. He's travelling with her urn

e. A black cat, a clover and a horseshoe

What does this mean?

A. He owns a farm

B. He's superstitious

C. He works with animals

Once you work out which of these statements are true and relevant, you realise there's only one cabin that can possibly be his.

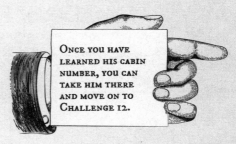

ONCE YOU HAVE LEARNED HIS CABIN NUMBER, YOU CAN TAKE HIM THERE AND MOVE ON TO CHALLENGE 12.

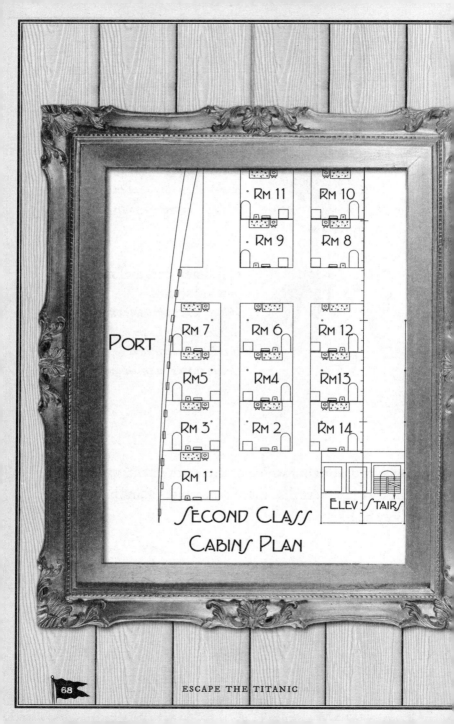

RM 11   RM 10

RM 9   RM 8

PORT

RM 7   RM 6   RM 12

RM5   RM4   RM13

RM 3   RM 2   RM 14

RM 1

ELEV STAIRS

SECOND CLASS
CABINS PLAN

There are only fourteen second-class cabins he could possibly mean. By eliminating the false and irrelevant statements about his tattoos you can eliminate the wrong ones, leaving one final possibility.

2ND CLASS ROOMS
1-14

ESCAPE THE TITANIC

Open the Hatch

As you carry the man into his cabin you notice two things about it: the hatch in the ceiling and a large number of clocks dotted about.

The water is beginning to get rather high in the room so you climb the ladder and try to open the hatch but it's locked, with three levers on its corners. Obviously, you will need to turn all three of the levers but you don't know whether to turn them left or right, and how many times. The man mumbles something about checking his diary. It's on the desk, open at his latest entry. He also points at the clocks and the map on the wall, indicating these are significant too.

London

New York City

Cape Town

San Francisco

Madrid

Santiago

ESCAPE THE TITANIC

The clocks show different times from all over the world. He must have been a very dedicated horologist to keep them updated like this while on the ship. Some of them are behind the current *Titanic* time and some of them are ahead of it. At first you think he wants you to set them all to the same time, which would be an impossible task before the water has reached the ceiling as you would have to turn each of them clockwise or anticlockwise. But then you realize the times are clues.

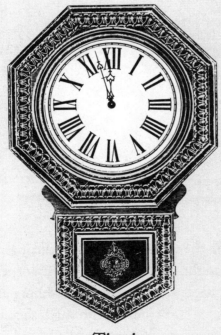

Titanic

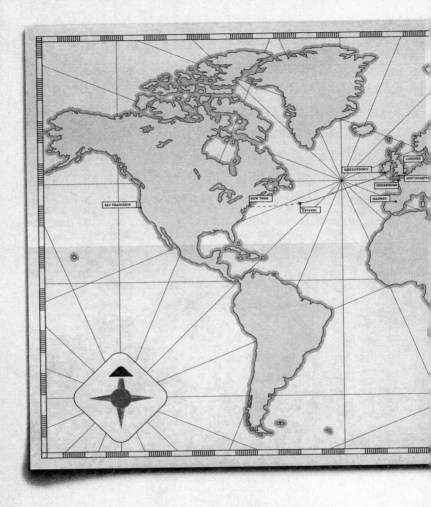

The map on the wall shows some of the locations he has visited, and the compass image in the corner has a very strange shape, reminiscent of something else you've seen. Perhaps his latest journal entry will shed light on the connections between the map, the clocks and the hatch.

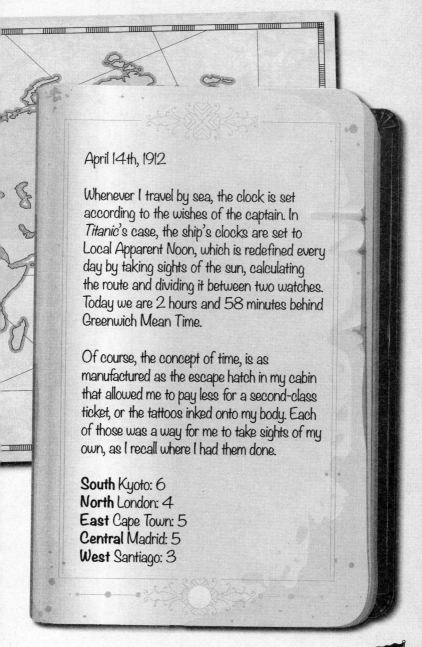

April 14th, 1912

Whenever I travel by sea, the clock is set according to the wishes of the captain. In *Titanic*'s case, the ship's clocks are set to Local Apparent Noon, which is redefined every day by taking sights of the sun, calculating the route and dividing it between two watches. Today we are 2 hours and 58 minutes behind Greenwich Mean Time.

Of course, the concept of time, is as manufactured as the escape hatch in my cabin that allowed me to pay less for a second-class ticket, or the tattoos inked onto my body. Each of those was a way for me to take sights of my own, as I recall where I had them done.

South Kyoto: 6
North London: 4
East Cape Town: 5
Central Madrid: 5
West Santiago: 3

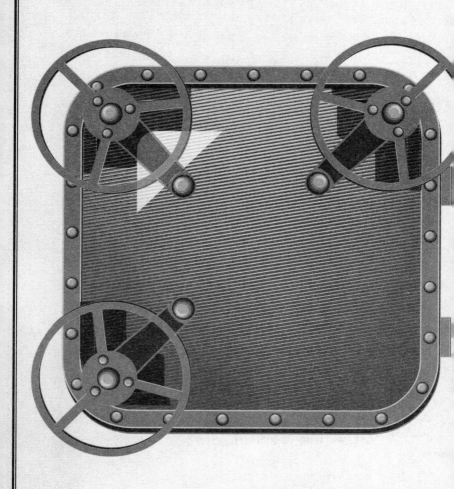

ESCAPE THE TITANIC

The handles are stiff, as apparently this hatch was probably only meant for emergencies and the ship's owners probably never thought it would be used. But if you know whether to turn them forwards or backwards and how many times, you should be able to open it and climb up to the next floor. The tattooed man groans on the bed where you put him as the water continues to rise. It's now or never.

WORK OUT THE DIRECTION AND NUMBER OF EACH HANDLE ROTATION TO OPEN THE HATCH AND PULL YOURSELF AND THE MAN UP THROUGH IT.

CHAPTER FOUR

— 13 —

Give Him a Haircut

You successfully climb up through the hatch, pulling the tattooed horologist with you. Reinvigorated by the exertion, he thanks you profusely, before running off.

You head in the opposite direction, relieved that this deck seems to be free of water, before wandering into a barber's shop. No sooner do you step inside than a desperate-looking man joins you. 'Ey mate, you're a barber, right? Listen, I've got two first-class tickets. I reckon they'll get us up to the top deck and into a lifeboat. But I don't really look the part,' he says, indicating his unkempt hair and beard. 'So if you make me look like a proper toff, I'll let you have one of these tickets.' You glance around the barber's shop. You can do this!

You have no idea how to cut hair. You did trim your dog's fur once when it fell into a gorse bush, though that probably won't help now. But the ticket could definitely help, and you find a book titled *F.P. Benshaw's Guide to Barbering*. You decide that what you need to find is an easy haircut that will:

a) allow him to go undetected in the first-class area
b) be the quickest to carry out

You're on a sinking ship, you don't have a lot of time and the man's panicked expression suggests he agrees. The book's cover shows the kind of equipment you need and luckily all the items are right in front of the mirror. You flick to a page of quick haircuts and the man barely glances at it, saying he's happy with any of them.

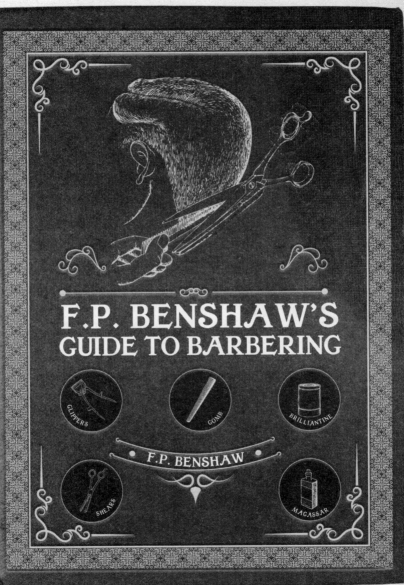

F.P. BENSHAW'S
GUIDE TO BARBERING

CLIPPERS

COMB

BRILLIANTINE

F.P. BENSHAW

SHEARS

MACASSAR

A: Clockwise Parting

An exciting new design. If you use shears, you'll find this takes one and a half times the time of the most 'aristocratic' haircut.

B: The Continental

This style takes the same amount of time as the other two fastest haircuts. However, you cannot use clippers.

C: The Baron

A little old-fashioned, both in its look and its use of macassar oil, but still a classic, and it only takes twice as long as it does to sterilize your equipment.

D: Hooray Henry

Still fashionable, and it is three times faster to do than the haircut with the celebrity name.

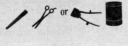

12

How long will it take to do each haircut? There are plenty of clues in the descriptions...

E: Dapper David

Looks complicated, but if you use clippers it's one third quicker to accomplish than the haircut that takes the longest.

F: Hello George

Surprisingly, this will take five times as long to cut as the most international haircut, even with the efficiency of using brilliantine.

G: The Peacock

Twice as quick to achieve as the haircut with the most timely name – and it ensures you stand out!

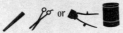

H: Basic Caruso

As long as you use the clippers, this tribute to the world-renowned tenor will take you three times the length of The Peacock to create. Otherwise, it takes the same time as the Dapper David.

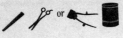

13

ONCE YOU HAVE WORKED OUT WHICH HAIRCUT IS THE QUICKEST AND MOST APPROPRIATE, YOU CAN CUT HIS HAIR AND MOVE ON TO CHALLENGE 14.

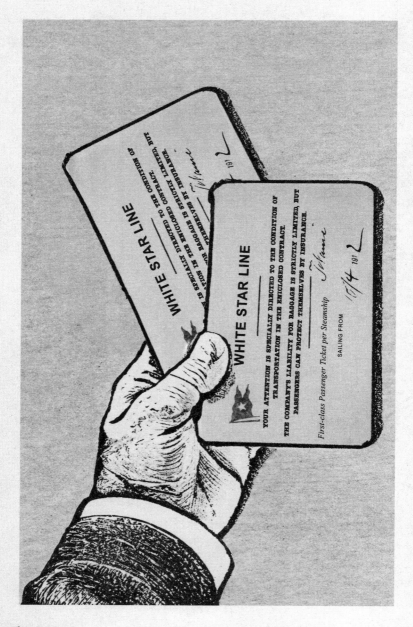

ESCAPE THE TITANIC

14

Stay Out of the Light

As soon as you complete the haircut and it looks plausible, you both charge out of the barber's shop with the tickets.

Guarding the corridor ahead of you are two stewards who are trying to prevent people rushing to the lifeboats. The electric lights are flickering on and off unnervingly. You confidently show one of them the tickets, which he examines closely before fixing you with an angry stare. 'These are fake!' he shouts. The man next to you immediately turns and runs off.

The other steward lunges for you but you evade him, running into a nearby corridor. Rather than give chase he stands guard at the centre, waiting for you to step into view again.

ESCAPE THE TITANIC

On. Off. On. Off. The lights change every second, blinking on and off in a regular metronomic rhythm. You can take advantage of the darkness to slip along the corridor unseen, but if you are standing *under* a light bulb when the lights come on, the steward will immediately attack you. It takes one second for you to take each step, except in places where water is seeping into the corridor, where it takes two seconds. You must find out which corridor will provide an escape: A, B, C or D. You are starting from the first space at the top of the corridor – not the stairs – and all the lights are *on*. You must keep moving.

FIND OUT WHICH
CORRIDOR IS THE
CORRECT ONE
TO ESCAPE TO
CHALLENGE 15.

ESCAPE THE TITANIC

15

Find the Right Tune

Somehow you manage to escape capture, though your heart is pounding — or is that the sound of the ship beginning to crack apart?

Looking desperately into the now abandoned second-class cabins you spot something strange: a cello! Perhaps you could use this to pretend to be a musician… You remember hearing there are two bands on board. You can't play a note, but you're prepared to bluff. Your recent luck holds out, and the moment you grab the cello you see a group of musicians running up the corridor.

They're heading up to the next deck to play music for the first-class passengers in an effort to keep them calm. 'I don't remember seeing your face before,' mutters one of the violinists.

'I was hired to be a backup,' you say quickly, 'but I wasn't needed.'

'Fine, come along. We've got to find our other violinist,' he says, marching off.

You figure that you stand more of a chance if you're with other musicians, so you follow them, hoping you can sneak off before you're required to play anything. One of them hands you a torn piece of a music sheet.

'Take a look at this,' he whispers in your ear cryptically, and then suddenly runs off.

'Strange man,' says the violinist, 'I think maybe he was just pretending to be a musician...'

'Terrible,' you say nervously.

'That's odd,' says the violinist peering at it.

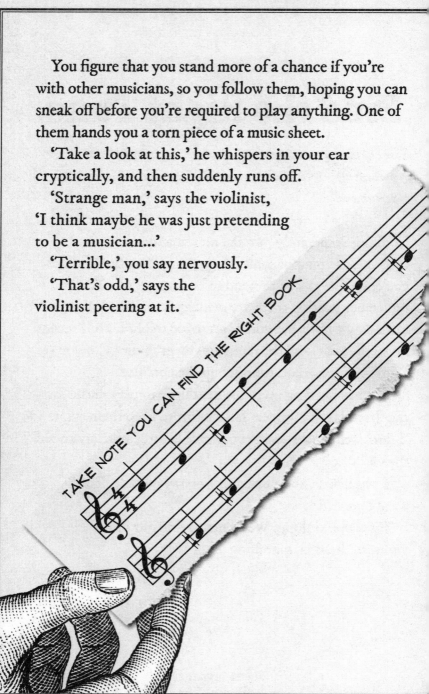

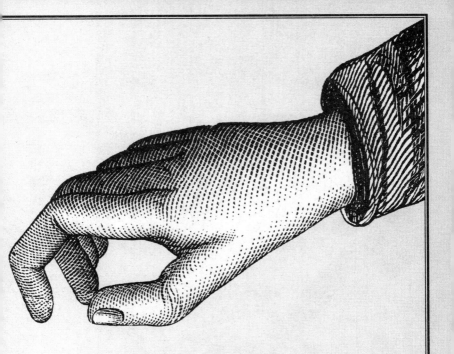

'That'd be a real racket if we ever tried to play it.'
Looking at the handwriting at the top, you suddenly
realize it's that of your old friend William Bailey. Was
that him just now? And why would he give you this?

ESCAPE THE TITANIC

'We'll play some of these,' says the violinist as you walk, showing you three pieces of sheet music. 'That weird guy gave us these but I've had a look inside and they seem legit, although there's a few scribbles inside them too...' Was your friend trying to send you a message, in his typically circuitous fashion?

Maybe the notes are a code similar to the enciphered words on the map he gave you, and they indicate one of these music scores: 'Maple Leaf Rag', 'Valse Septembre', or 'Nearer My God to Thee'? You try counting the number of notes to see if they match the letters in the

names, but it's difficult to tell because the page is torn. Anyway, you can't read music and don't know the names of the notes, so you'll need a bit of logical thinking to work this one out. You notice that some of the notes are the same, so perhaps that could help you find a pattern and work out which song it is.

FIND OUT WHICH PIECE OF MUSIC CONTAINS WILLIAM'S MESSAGE TO MOVE TO CHALLENGE 16.

 94

16

Answer the Questions

Inside the music score there is a message instructing you to meet in a particular location on C Deck. You can only hope you manage to get that far.

A little further along, the violinist spots a figure approaching and says 'Ah, there's the other fiddler. We met him about five minutes ago.' You turn to see a familiar menacing silhouette.

It's Sharp! That bounder who left you for dead on lower G Deck!

He's clutching a violin and giving you his most insidious smile. You have to hold back from shouting at him or grabbing him, knowing that it would probably blow your cover, but you give him a jolly good glare anyway.

He joins the group and as you walk along you whisper, 'You trapped me, I nearly drowned!'

'And yet here you are,' he whispers back, casually. 'Perhaps you are smarter than I thought. Smart enough to know that if you expose me, I will expose you too.'

He is right. You are forced to be temporary teammates. 'But you'll run into more trouble up there unless you can get your story straight.' He says seriously. 'You will need to convince the crewmen guarding the stairs and corridors that you are a genuine passenger. I'm Sharp – and you need to be too.'

He starts to ask you questions about the ship and the voyage so far, saying that they are the facts you will need to know in order to pass yourself off as a fare-paying traveller. You suspect it is another kind of cruel joke but at this point you have no alternative but to reply!

1. *How many people are on board?*
a) *3,121*
b) *2,224*
c) *1,986*

2. *Who built the Titanic?*
a) *Harland & Wolff*
b) *Swan Hunter & Wigham Richardson*
c) *Hawthorne Leslie & Co.*

3. *What was the final port before setting sail to New York?*
a) *Cherbourg*
b) *Southampton*
c) *Queenstown*

4. Titanic has struck an iceberg. What are icebergs made of?
a) Rock
b) Ice
c) Burgers

7. Who is the captain of this ship?
a) Edward Smith
b) James Hook
c) There is no captain

5. In which direction does one pass the port at dinner?
a) Left
b) Right
c) Forwards

8. What is my first name?
a) James
b) Philip
c) Unknown

6. How would you address the Queen if you met her?
a) Queen Mary
b) Queen Victoria
c) Your Majesty

9. Which of these questions cannot be answered?
a) 8. Because he has no first name
b) 5. Because port is not served at dinner.
c) 1. Because it's unknown how many stowaways there are.

ANSWER SHARP'S
QUESTIONS
CORRECTLY TO
ESCAPE UPWARDS
TO THE NEXT DECK.

CHAPTER FIVE

SALOON (D) DECK

17

Mix a Cocktail

You run up the stairs to the Saloon (D) Deck, accompanied by the odious Sharp. Suddenly you find yourself in the First-Class Lounge. The ship has begun to make horrifying creaking and groaning noises. While some passengers are panicking, others are seemingly resigned to their fate. In one of the chairs, a sinister-looking gentleman sits puffing on a cigar as if he didn't have a care in the world.

Sharp pushes you forward.

'Mr. Demone, I've brought you a waiter who will prepare you a cocktail while we secure your place on the lifeboat.'

You pull Sharp to one side and whisper to him that you have no idea how to make drinks.

He grins nastily. 'Doesn't matter. Just go to the drinks storage next to the smoking room and figure something out. I'll do the rest, then you can go on your way. Or do you want me to expose you?'

You have no choice, so you ask Demone for his order.
He glares at you.

'Just make me somethin' from the menu, quick.
And don't try to fob me off with some random mixture –
I want a proper cocktail.'

You look at Sharp. 'Here's today's specials,' he hisses, passing you a piece of paper.

Reading the recipes as you walk to the drinks storage, you decided that you'll just make whatever is easiest with the available ingredients.

Cocktail Recipes

Old Fashioned

- 2 tsp sugar syrup
- a dash or two of Angostura Bitters
- a splash of water
- 2 oz Scotch whisky or bourbon
- soda water (optional)
- an orange slice
- a maraschino cherry (optional)

Tuxedo

- a dash of maraschino
- a dash of absinthe
- two dashes of orange bitters
- 1½ oz gin
- 1½ oz dry vermouth

Gibson

- 2½ oz gin
- ½ oz dry vermouth
- cocktail onion

Tom Collins

- a splash of soda water
- 2 oz gin
- ¾ oz fresh lemon juice
- ½ oz sugar syrup
- orange/maraschino cherry flag, for garnish

But when you get to the drinks storage you find that the labels on the bottles have all become smudged. How can you work out which is which? There's a lemon on one of the bottles, so that must be the lemon juice. And you can just make out an 'AB' on another, so that must be the Angostura Bitters. At the back of the cupboard is a small card with a symbol on it for each of the bottles. You can use that to work out which bottle is which: the symbols must relate to different characteristics of the bottles.

Eventually you realize there's only one cocktail you can make...

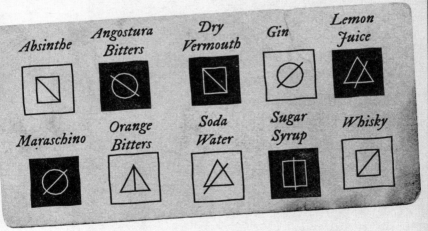

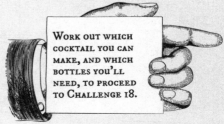

WORK OUT WHICH COCKTAIL YOU CAN MAKE, AND WHICH BOTTLES YOU'LL NEED, TO PROCEED TO CHALLENGE 18.

18

Turn the Tables

Once you've mixed the cocktail you begin carrying it over to Mr. Demone, but Sharp grabs your arm and brings you around the corner.

Pulling out some kind of vial, he goes to pour a few drops of some liquid into the cocktail, but you pull it back from his reach.

'Is that... poison?' You say angrily.

Sharp rolls his eyes. 'It's a sleeping draught. It'll make him a little bit tired, is all.' You shake your head. 'On a sinking ship? That's a death sentence!'

Sharp looks around nervously. 'Keep your voice down! Listen, Mel Demone is a bad egg, and the world would be better off without him. Or would you rather I introduce you personally? I'm sure he'd love to meet a stowaway...'

You consider this.

Then, in one swift movement, you throw the cocktail glass to the floor, where it immediately smashes. You may be a stowaway, but you are not a murderer!

Sharp gives you a look of pure hatred. You have outwitted him this time, but he has another plan up his sleeve. He abruptly grabs Demone by the arm and loudly accuses you of planning to poison him.

Everyone in the room immediately turns, and Demone leaps to his feet and shouts for his bodyguards. Sharp uses the disturbance to make a break for it, giving you a sneer as he exits the room at speed.

You're going to have to run, but at that moment the ship lurches and all the lights in the room go out. How can you find your way to the door?

You find what you think must be the layout plan, although it is barely visible in the moonlight. It is a 10 x 15 grid showing the positions of the tables, but it is blank! However, you can work out where the tables are placed by looking at the numbers at the sides of the grid. The numbers indicate how many adjacent tables are in each row and column. Individual numbers have a gap of at least one square between them: fill in the grid...

	7 2	9 3	2 2 2	2 2 2	2 2 2	2 2 2	2 2 2	2 2 2	15	7 5
8										
10										
2 2										
2 2										
2 2										
2 2										
2 2										
10										
8										
2										
2										
2										
2 2										
10										
8										

Puzzle board (nonogram):

	1 1	2 1	3 1	1 6	1 10	1 1 6	1 10	1 1 6	1 10	1 1 6	1 10	1 1 6	1 10	1 1 5	1 3 1	3 1
1 1 1 1 1																
1 1 1 1 1																
1 1 1 1 1																
1 1 1 1																
1 1 1 1																
1 1 1 1																
1 1 1 1																
?																
15																
14																
13																
10																
15																
0																
0																

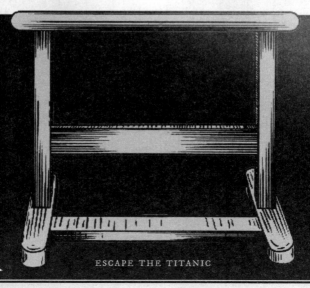

ESCAPE THE TITANIC

As you work out the positions of the tables, the image that emerges makes you realize that this can't possibly be the seating plan. At that moment you spot another grid mounted on a board nearby, also without markings, but this time missing one key element needed to interpret it. That must be the real table plan, but the previous one will help you solve the second. You also remember seeing a notice announcing that the tables had been arranged in a particular pattern to commemorate *Titanic*'s maiden voyage which may prove useful.

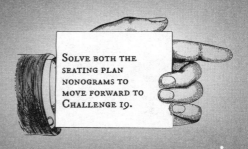

SOLVE BOTH THE
SEATING PLAN
NONOGRAMS TO
MOVE FORWARD TO
CHALLENGE 19.

ESCAPE THE TITANIC

19

Find a Friend

Escaping through the door, you find you've finally reached the bottom of the Grand Staircase. Despite the current situation, you can still admit its design is impressive.
A group of stewards are shepherding first-class passengers up the stairs in the direction of the lifeboats. They're trying to concentrate on women and children, but are taking anyone they can in the general confusion.

'Vivian! Over here!' shouts someone. A crew member notices you and marches over.

'You're not a waiter!' he fumes. 'Why are you wearing that outfit?'

You nervously claim that you were hired at the last minute. He turns red with fury.

'I am the purser, and I know everyone who has been hired onto this crew.'

That's a blow.

As he glares at you and the crowd turn to look, you have to think faster than ever before.

Suddenly you remember something. You'd read about Vivian Ducksbury-Bail, a self-declared philanthropist, who wrote a series of letters to *The Times* promising to help any stowaway on board. It's a long-shot but worth a try – if only you could identify Vivian in the crowd.

Monday, April 8th

Sir,

In a matter of days, I will embark on 'Titanic's' maiden voyage, and plan to use the journey to enlighten my fellow passengers.

My hat, made by a poor milliner from Spitalfields, will not be removed, even if it conceals the close-cropped haircut given to me by an impoverished barber from Bow. I will not smile when in First Class. And if you see me weeping, it is out of pity for the working man's natural plight and not because of an extreme bout of summer catarrh – which is so extreme that I cannot even look at a flower.

Yes, I shall be aboard, and should I meet a true stowaway I would run to their aid!

Yours,

Vivian Ducksbury-Bail

Monday, April 10th

Sir,

I was displeased to note that alongside your salutary article about the 'Titanic's ongoing construction there was a screed castigating the poor. I adjusted my spectacles in the hope I had been mistaken, but I was not!

Do you not see that we are all together on this ship we call life, even if some of us are in Third Class, or even stowaways below decks.

We must remember that the bowler worn frequently by many gentlemen in the City of London was once the preferred headgear of the honest Irishman. The bow tie was once the garb of the noble Croats in the 1600s! Even my unfashionably long hair, associated with the Cavaliers, was also the required style of the ascetic or hermit. Without the working man, there would be no 'Titanic'!

Yours,
Vivian Ducksbury-Bail

Despite all the clues they contain, the two letters seem to contradict each other, and it is difficult to get a clear idea of what Vivian Ducksbury-Bail looks like, or even if they are a man or a woman.

ESCAPE THE TITANIC

In one letter the writer says they have had their hair cut short, but in the other one they claim to have long hair. Perhaps if you could work out which letter was written first, you could compile an up-to-date description of their appearance?

There are thirty people in the room. By a process of elimination you should be able to work out which one is Vivian Ducksbury-Bail, assuming you have correctly noted that description.

Hurry up, though. The crowd are starting to point accusatory fingers at you, and the only person who can help you out is Vivian Ducksbury-Bail!

CHOOSE THE CORRECT PERSON TO MOVE ON TO CHALLENGE 20.

ESCAPE THE TITANIC

20

Help the Doctor

Waving to Vivian Ducksbury-Bail, you successfully mime that you're a stowaway. At once, they march over to the purser and vouch for you, stating that you are his personal steward. Begrudgingly the purser allows you and a small group to pass. Among those heading up the stairs, an old lady trips and falls. Her leg is very visibly broken! A man rushes up, he is apparently a doctor.

'Looks nasty... I wish I had my bag with me. I'll have to fix it battlefield style.' He turns to you, and orders you to get the following items from the people here:

- *a long piece of wood to act as a splint*
- *something to secure the splint, such as a scarf*
- *some bandages*
- *some water to bathe the wound*
- *some kind of alcohol – pain relief for her, I should add.*

The numbers of the items are:

Splint		Scarf	
Bandages		Water	
Alcohol			

Now that you know who has the items you need, you just need to work out how to reach them. Looking around the space, you realize the shifting furniture and panicking passengers have left you limited paths to move along. You must find the path that leads you to all five items and the people who have them.

ESCAPE THE TITANIC

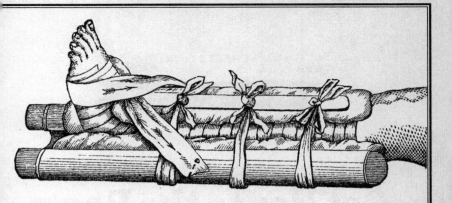

You remember the crowd of people from the previous puzzle. Make your way through the maze of furniture, boxes, cases and people. If someone is friendly (smiling) they will let you pass, but if they are not you will need to find another route.

FIND THE ROUTE TO COLLECT THE ITEMS, HELP THE DOCTOR AND ASCEND THE GRAND STAIRCASE TO THE NEXT DECK.

CHAPTER SIX

SHELTER (C) DECK

—— 21 ——

Get Her to the Room

*As you escort the woman up the Grand Staircase you become
horribly aware of the ship's lurching movements, as are the
panicking people around you. What chance do you possibly
have of getting to a lifeboat?*

As if reading your mind the woman whispers, 'I know
you're a stowaway! I saw you talking to Vivian... he
looked so excited to be helping you. Well, I want to help
you too. My name's Clemmie Finsdale. I'll get you on a
lifeboat. You can be my attendant.

You can hardly believe your luck... 'But first,' she adds,
'you must help my acquaintance.' Your smile freezes.

'We came on board together, but he's barely left
his room. He's sick, I know, but he won't admit it.
Help me to retrieve him and I'll be your ticket off
this boat.'

Supporting her weight, you help Clemmie down the corridor. She is just explaining that her friend is Myron Nithercott, the famous archaeologist, when the ship's centre of gravity shifts dramatically, and you almost lose hold of her.

You're having serious difficulty balancing during these sudden lurches and you're losing valuable time.

'What if we use these bags to balance ourselves?' she suggests. 'I can hold one with my good arm, and you can hold another on the other side. But they will both need to be of equal weight.' You quickly gather some nearby items and find a combination that balances.

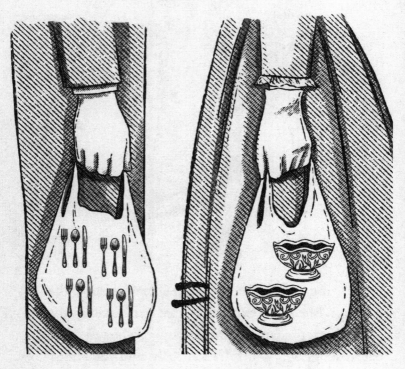

Four sets of cutlery = two silver bowls.

 ESCAPE THE TITANIC

Arm in arm with Clemmie, each holding a bag of items, the pair of you stagger forward a few paces. But the bags aren't heavy enough, and soon spill and scatter everywhere. You quickly gather up some of them but are forced to use a couple of nearby silver candelabras in order to compensate.

'I'm fairly certain this isn't their intended use,' groans Clemmie, grimacing in pain.

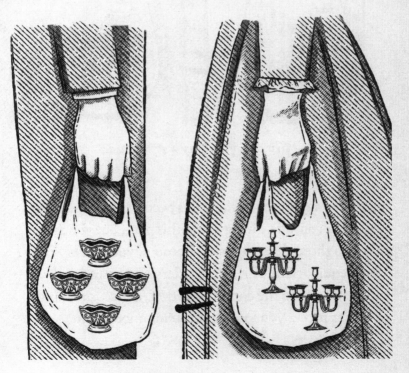

Four silver bowls = two candelabras.

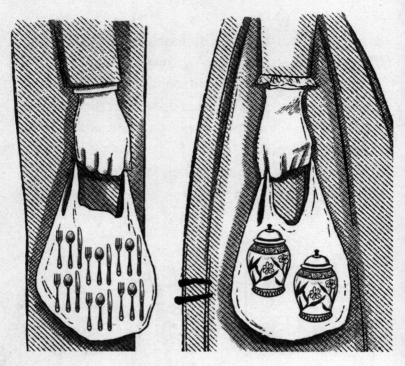

Six sets of cutlery = two vases.

Before long, however, the items become dislodged and lost. You consider giving up on this plan, but you are so close to the archaeologist's stateroom, you quickly find some equilibrium with some cutlery and vases.

As you round the corner, however, a loud, creaking shudder makes you lose all the items once again.

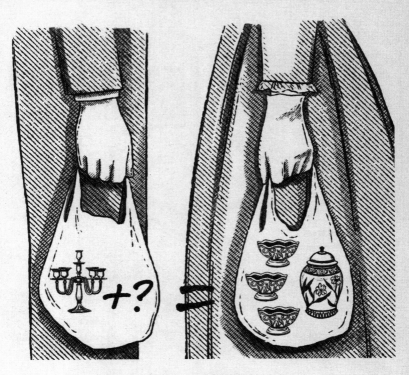

One candelabra + ? sets of cutlery
= one vase and three silver bowls.

This is your last chance. Clemmie has put three bowls and a vase into her bag. You only have a candelabra and some cutlery.

How many sets of cutlery do you need to balance out Clemmie's bag?

WORK OUT HOW MANY CUTLERY SETS ARE REQUIRED TO MOVE ON TO CHALLENGE 22.

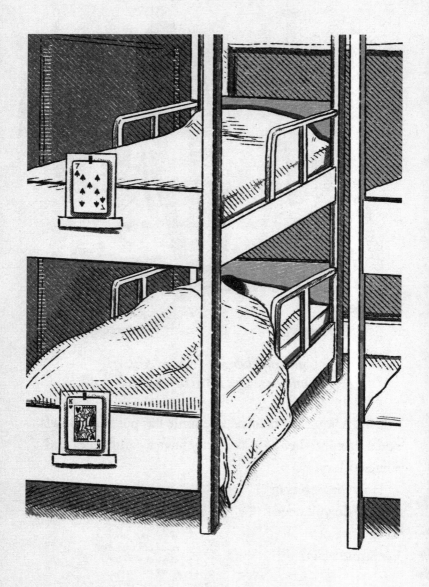

22

Find His File

*You arrive at the room of Myron Nithercott, archaeologist,
but as you go to knock, a nearby attendant stops you. 'He's
not in there. They took him to the hospital!' he informs you.*

A hospital on board? Luckily it is not far away. When you
arrive you find that it is dimly lit, with only two patients
in the beds. Clemmie has to sit down, closing her eyes
with pain. She's unable to help, so you approach the beds.

'Oi! What d'you think you're doing?' shouts a seated
figure near by. He appears to be a steward, and is
apparently quite drunk. He starts moving towards you.

'We're here to see Myron Nithercott,' you say.

'I don't know their names,' he growls.

'Aren't they written on their bedside notes?'

'No, just playing cards. I think it was a game they were
doing. I'm just here to watch them and make sure no one
talks to them.'

'But the ship is sinking!'

'It can't be. It's unsinkable. They'll sort it out. They
know what they're doing. Now clear off!'

You're tempted to simply grab Myron and escort him
out, but which one is he? Unfortunately Clemmie is now
delirious with pain and cannot help you.

Maybe if you can find Myron Nithercott's file you can work out which patient he is. But how do you find it when all you have is a playing card? You notice a file on the table with the name Charles Petherbridge. It is marked 'D7'. You look at the playing cards, the filing cabinet files and Petherbridge's file, and work out which draw to open. When you have Nithercott and the file, you go back to his room...

Petherbridge

Myron

ESCAPE THE TITANIC

FILES ARE IN ALPHABETICAL ORDER

FIND OUT THE LETTER AND NUMBER OF MYRON NITHERCOTT'S FILE TO MOVE ON TO CHALLENGE 23.

23

Open the Box

You escort Nithercott and Clemmie back to his room. The study is packed with archaeological treasures from around the world, and there are texts and images pinned to the walls. Back in his own bed, Nithercott still seems delirious. He points to a box and a game of dominoes on the table.

'Open... the... box!' he croaks.

The box seems to have four regular indentations in the lid, each of which fits a single domino. Each slot has an arrow pointing in a different direction. But which domino fits in which slot?

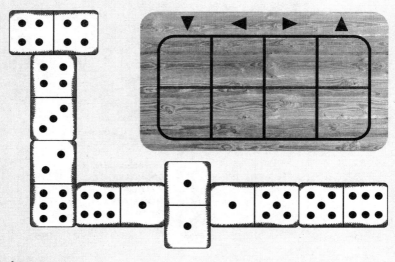

Nithercott now gestures in the direction of some small shields hanging on the wall. They look like Viking figures.

'Oh yes, his favourites,' says Clemmie. 'The four chieftains. Those markings on them are runes, but I don't know what they mean or in what order they go. I think some of them might be upside down, though I believe they still have the same meaning.'

The Saga of the Four Winds

three –

King Sven had four sons: Arvid One-tooth,
Magnus Single-fang, Erik the Half-sighted
and Ragnar Lone-eye.

On his deathbed he made them swear that they
would separate the kingdom into four – North,
South, East and West – for if they ever fought
among themselves, the kingdom would be
thrown into chaos.

Arvid, the eldest and most level-headed, said
he would have the North, for it was the largest.

Erik, who was missing his right eye, said he
would take the West, but Magnus and Ragnar
objected to Erik having the West. Arvid then
said that he would take the West. Ragnar, the
youngest, volunteered to the take the South, as
it was the smallest, but Erik said he wanted it
for its fine hunting grounds. Erik refused the
East as it was a wild place where he had lost
his right eye. Magnus said he would not take
it either, as he had lost all but his left tooth
there.

In the end though, all the brothers
were happy, and ruled well.

one –

You notice a typewritten story on the desk.

'One of those interminable Icelandic sagas about Viking chieftains...' says Clemmie. 'Although, maybe it relates to the shields on the wall. And look, it tells us the values for some of the runes.'

Reading the saga carefully, you can find out which shield represents which son, and which region of their land they ruled over. This will let you decipher the runes and put the correct dominoes in the lid of the box.

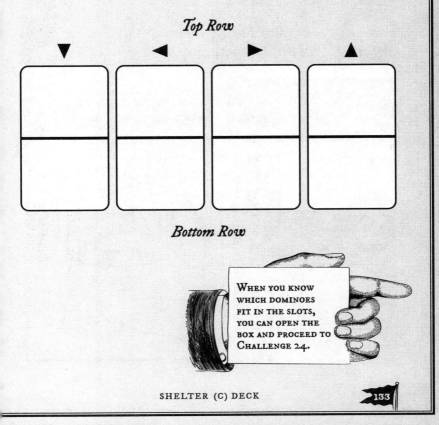

Top Row

Bottom Row

WHEN YOU KNOW WHICH DOMINOES FIT IN THE SLOTS, YOU CAN OPEN THE BOX AND PROCEED TO CHALLENGE 24.

Solve the Mystery

With the correct dominoes in position, a hidden mechanism embedded in the box's lid whirs and the clasp clicks open. You gingerly lift the lid, half expecting to find an elixir or other drug, only to find... a piece of paper with symbols on it.

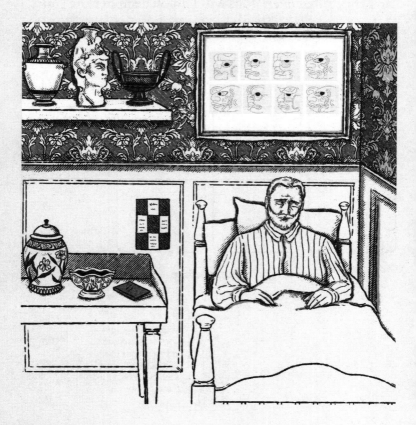

'Oh, Myron! You and your puzzles!' exclaims Clemmie, with some affection. 'Let me see that!' You pass her the slip of paper. She holds it up close to her face.

'These are myroglyphs,' she explains, pointing to one of the charts on the wall. 'Apparently he uses them all the time. They're his own versions of Mayan symbols. I've no idea how to decode them.'

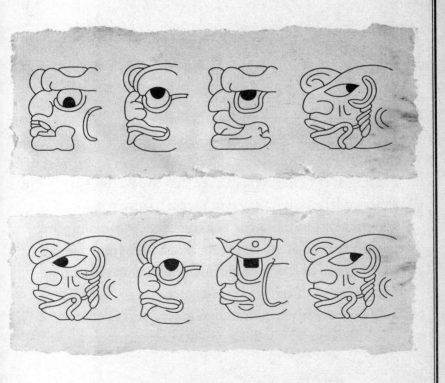

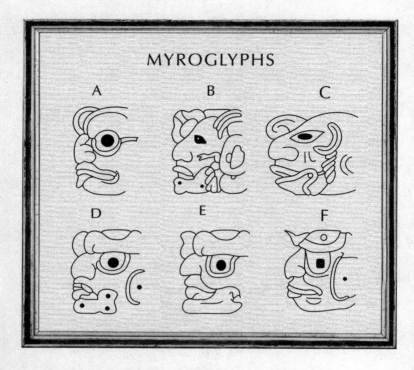

MYROGLYPHS

A   B   C

D   E   F

Peering at the chart you can see that the symbols are assigned letters, but they don't seem to give you a comprehensible message. There must be something else needed to read them. Glancing around the room you also spot a group of four strange notes pinned on the wall in categories, with arrows at the centre.

'Those are his memorandum notes,' says Clemmie. 'He's always making them, yet never remembers a thing...'

Useful words

A – THE
B – AN
C – OF
D – AND
E – LARGE
F – SMALL

Correspondence

A – REPLIED
B – REPLY
C – IGNORE
D – DISPOSE
E – ANALYSE
F – BURN

Expenses

A – TICKET
B – ROOM
C – BOOKS
D – STEWARD
E – MEDICINE
F – DINNER

Archaeology

A – SPECULATE
B – LOCATE
C – QUESTION
D – FOLLOW
E – PROCURE
F – ARCHIVE

These notes, combined with the chart, allow you to decode the slip of paper in the box and you end up with a cryptic message. But what does it mean?

Suddenly Myron sits up in bed, seemingly lucid.

'Take me to the library!' he gasps. Noticing Clemmie's injured leg, he realizes you'll have to escort both of them.

The ship's library is small but well stocked. You notice that several of the books have strange lines on their spines. As soon as they arrive, Myron and Clemmie collapse into a large chair, holding each other close, clearly wanting to make the most of the little time they have left together.

'I think we shall remain here,' says Myron, taking a volume on Egyptian history from the shelf.

'I'm sorry we can't get you to a lifeboat,' says Clemmie, regretfully; your heart sinks.

'But we can help you – remember my message,' whispers Myron, pointing at the bookshelf.

SHELTER (C) DECK

It's clear that the message in the box relates to this room, but what does it mean? Water begins to seep into the room, but you notice that it is vanishing through a crack under the bookshelf. Could there be a passage?

'Do I need to pull one of these books out?' you ask Myron, who is clearly distracted.

'The journey begins at the base of the spear,' replies Myron with a smile. Despite the circumstances, he is clearly reluctant to spoil his final puzzle.

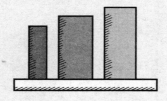

The books are all different sizes. Perhaps the lines join up in some way?

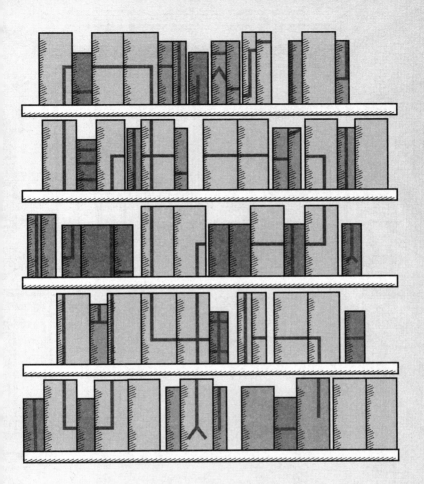

WHEN YOU HAVE FOUND
THE CORRECT BOOK YOU
CAN OPEN THE SECRET
PASSAGE AND FIND
THE STAIRS THAT
WILL TAKE YOU UP
TO THE NEXT DECK.

ESCAPE THE TITANIC

CHAPTER SEVEN

BRIDGE (B) DECK

—— 25 ——

Disguise Yourself

As you ascend a ladder in the strange, dark passage, you wonder where you will emerge. Sliding a wooden panel to one side, you find yourself confronted by shirts and hangers, and you realize that you're inside a wardrobe.

Peering through the gap in the wardrobe doors, you see that it's one of the first-class staterooms, and there is no one about. You carefully enter the room and reason you must be on B Deck, but you barely have time to get your bearings before a frantic knocking comes at the door. 'Excuse me sir? We must get to the lifeboats immediately!'

The tone suggests that he's not your usual steward. Suddenly your eye alights on a framed photograph on the bedside table: this must be the room's occupant.

It occurs to you that fate has given you the opportunity to disguise yourself as this person, if only you could find and put on the items he wears:

- *glasses*
- *jacket*
- *straw hat*
- *beard*
- *bow tie*

You notice his open diary on the desk, perhaps this will give you clues to where you can find some of the items.

'Live your art!' Kate always tells me. Tedious. Very well, I shall organize my room according the emotional resonance that each object affords me. Then when I'm late for a rendez-vous, I can say I'm living my art!

She reminds me of Father, criticizing my deficiencies. But Father did not speak of art, only my eyesight, my dark complexion, even my 'weak facial hair', no match for his famous moustache. I pretend I no longer care but the itchiness of this fake beard says otherwise. I like to think he would be enraged about where I have placed my spare whiskers, though.

When Father spoke of France it was with hatred and venom. And yet it was there that I found my calling as an artist, and also this lovely straw hat. It reminds me of that country and the freedom it represents for me.

The art in this cabin is abysmal, but every time I take it down the steward rehangs it, so it must remain.

The same is true of that damnable hand bell that aggravates Gauguin so. At least there is an ashtray. I wish Kate would not leave her palette and brush in here. She knows I abhor the smell of paint and linseed oil in such confined quarters. I ensured my own composition was fully dried before I hung it. But it has now become part of my room's design and I cannot bear for it to be moved.

Once my sponsor and I meet my contact on board I look forward to putting this whole business behind me and simply getting on with my art.

AT

He has also written instructions for the care of his parrot. Perhaps this will also give some clues.

NOTES FOR THE CARE OF GAUGUIN

1. He sleeps nineteen hours a day. The room cannot be too bright. If he sees any kind of light during his sleep he will become agitated. You should use his striped cage cover to allow him a small amount of stimulation, although I fear the stripes on the cover I brought might be overstimulating.
2. He can only eat very fine millet. No nuts or anything larger than a lentil. His digestion is extremely sensitive.
3. He loves to steal eyeglasses, so do not wear any around him. This is particularly irksome to me as I am especially myopic, and my eyeglasses are key to me liberation from the fog of confusion that my life once was.
4. He is mortally afraid of bow ties, which again annoys me as I love their shape, reminiscent as it is of certain timepieces.
5. Despite his many flaws I love him dearly, so please treat him with the utmost care. All other birds are abominable to me.
6. He also hates rugs. So no rugs.

Arthur Tisdale

You spot what must be Tisdale's painting, though something doesn't seem quite right about it.

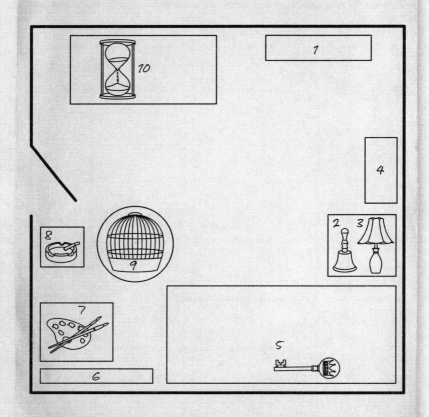

ESCAPE THE TITANIC

Some of the details of the painting seem significant, particularly when you see the floor plan of the room that he has drawn and his annotations.

1. Father's portrait
2. Hand bell (do not ring)
3. Bed lamp
4. Paris poster
5. Key to Paris
6. Horrible dove painting
7. Kate's palette and brushes
8. Ashtray
9. Gauguin's cage
10. Hourglass

It seems as if he required these items to be in particular places in his room. But why hasn't he included that stripy rug? Now you must work out where the five disguise details you need are kept or hidden.

ONCE YOU HAVE
WORKED OUT THE
FIVE LOCATIONS OF
THE ITEMS, YOU
CAN PUT ON YOUR
DISGUISE AND GO ON
TO CHALLENGE 26.

26

Find the Errors

Wearing the five disguise items you have found, you push open the door and greet the steward. Except it's not a steward! It's a furious-looking gentleman.

'Tisdale!' he growls, grabbing your lapels. 'You owe me fifty pounds! And if you haven't got it, you'll be trying your luck on a long swim to New York.' He is surprisingly strong for such a wiry man.

'I'm... I'm not Tisdale,' you splutter.

'Of course you aren't,' says the man sarcastically, releasing you. 'You just happen to be in his room, wearing his clothes and matching his picture.' He gestures towards the photograph of Tisdale. You consider removing your disguise but that would probably cause even more trouble.

'These pictures you sent me each have three mistakes!' he shouts, waving four pieces of paper at you. 'How can you expect people to believe these forgeries are the real thing if they have basic errors?' You take the pictures from him, seeing that they are well executed line drawings done with ink.

BRIDGE (B) DECK

'When I agreed to fund this endeavour, I did not expect to be sent flawed images!' he continues to sputter. You realize he must be the 'sponsor' that Tisdale mentioned in his diary.

'Didn't I send you a note with these?' you ask, buying some time to think.

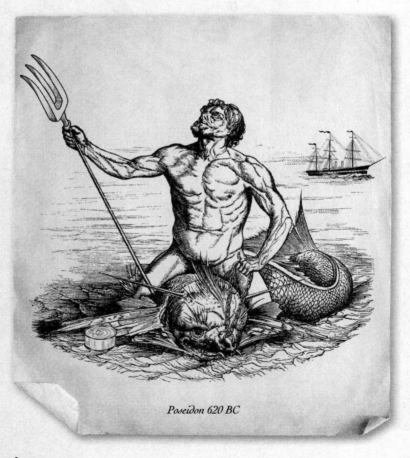

Poseidon 620 BC

'You did. Some nonsense about the common mistake telling me the meeting place to get the real pictures. I don't have time for these games!' shouts the man, looking like he's about to grab you again.

You suspect that Tisdale had intended to convey to this man the location of the meeting on board the ship without alerting anyone else, due to the clandestine nature of their association. You realize you must quickly work out the location you both have to visit before this man really loses his temper and things get ugly.

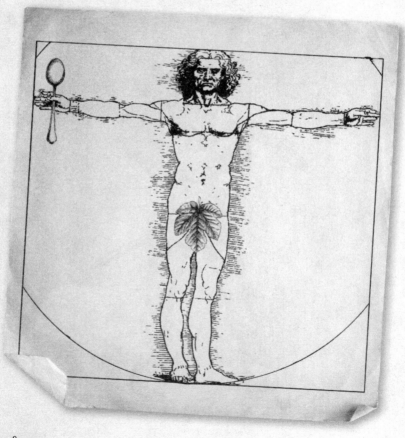

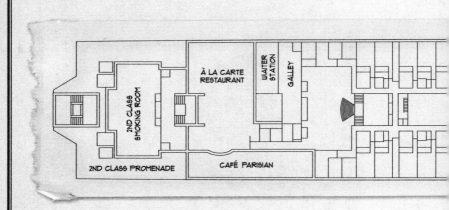

It would help to be able to narrow it down. You suddenly remember that you saw another short note on Tisdale's desk. You retrieve it and find it's a list of places located on B Deck.

Private Promenade
Second-class Smoking Room
À la Carte Restaurant
Waiter station
~~My cabin~~

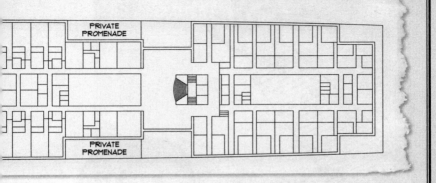

One of these must be the location indicated by the pictures. But what is the common clue in the pictures?

FIND ALL TWELVE ERRORS IN THE PAINTINGS AND THE COMMON ELEMENT THAT REVEALS THE LOCATION OF THE MEETING.

ESCAPE THE TITANIC

27

Decode the Message

Once you tell him the location of the meeting, he seems a little mollified and the two of you make your way there. You plan to break away from him at the first opportunity but he makes it clear that escape is not a possibility, and you both arrive at the location to meet Tisdale's connection.

Your blood runs cold when you see his face: it's that bounder Sharp! He smiles nastily. You sense he immediately sees through your disguise, as he turns to the angry man and says 'Colonel Frostrup, would you be so kind as to go and get us all a drink?' The Colonel seems astonished at this imposition but complies 'in the interest of business' and once he's gone Sharp fixes you with a penetrating stare.

'I was expecting a forger, not a forgery,' hisses Sharp. 'Why the deuce are you wearing Tisdale's clothes and beard? I imagine the fool must be passed out in a bar somewhere. No matter, I doubt I'll need his skills once I procure the item I'm looking for on board.'

You stand up in the hope of making a swift exit, but Sharp produces his knife from under the table, and holds it to your stomach.

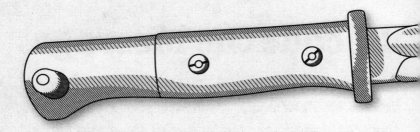

'I should just turn you over to the stewards. But you have an opportunity to assist me once again, and I suggest you take it. Let's go for a walk on the deck before our friend the Colonel returns with those drinks.'

Outside it is cold and dark. A few confused passengers mill around wearing life vests but they pay you no regard. Sharp forces you to sit on a bench.

'I was lucky enough to get a second chance to catch up with our friend, the now late Mr. Demone. And after I'd wiped his blood from my little blade here, I retrieved this rather pretty object...'

He shows you an ornate key decorated with a crown.

'Remember the bag you helped me retrieve earlier?'

'The one belonging to your "brother"?' you ask dryly.

'The same. It contains an item I need to acquire. But the key to open it was stolen by Demone's men, so I've been in a bit of a rush trying to get my hands on it. However, this key does not open the bag's lock.' He now reveals two pieces of paper.

'I found these on Demone as well. Apologies if this one's a little blood-stained. I can make neither head nor tail of them, but I remember now you're rather good at riddles.'

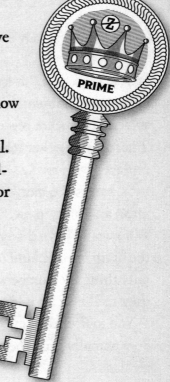

The first piece of paper seems to be a string of numbers in a telegram. You remember the ciphers from earlier...

TELEGRAM RECEIVED

71-19-11/31-11-97/71-19-2-71
47-53-11-43-67/71-19-11/3-2-17
23-67/23-43/71-19-11/5-61-47-83-67/43-11-67-71

'Yes, it's in code. I'm not a fool.' Sharp replies to your unspoken comment. 'But without the code key it can't be solved! The other piece of paper is a grid with 1–100 on it. There are no other markings, but the number 89 has been replaced with an X.

'X marks the spot,' Sharp says sourly, 'but it doesn't mean anything to me. There isn't even an 89 on the note. Who would have thought a thug like Demone would have the brain for this kind of tomfoolery?' You notice that the only thing the numbers on the note have in common is they're almost all odd numbers.

You look at the key with its decoration and realize it does actually hold the answer to how to decipher this message.

1	**2**	**3**	4	**5**	6	**7**	8	9	10
11	12	**13**	14	15	16	**17**	18	**19**	20
21	22	**23**	24	25	26	27	28	**29**	30
31	32	33	34	35	36	**37**	38	39	40
41	42	**43**	44	45	46	**47**	48	49	50
51	52	**53**	54	55	56	57	58	**59**	60
61	62	63	64	65	66	**67**	68	69	70
71	72	**73**	74	75	76	77	78	**79**	80
81	82	**83**	84	85	86	87	88	X	90
91	92	93	94	95	96	**97**	98	99	100

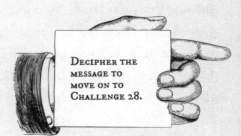

DECIPHER THE
MESSAGE TO
MOVE ON TO
CHALLENGE 28.

28

Fight Sharp

Sharp keeps his knife close to you as you decipher the message, and when you reveal the answer he curses.

'Ridiculous! That cannot be true!' He puts the key and the paper back in his pocket. The nasty look in his eyes suggests you have outlived your usefulness to him.

A steward happens to be passing, so in desperation you call out: 'Help, he's got a knife!' The steward runs over. Sharp curses and quickly hides his blade, but you are sure the steward will want to apprehend this criminal. Instead, he bows deferentially.

'Oh, it's you, Viscount Sharp. I'm terribly sorry to interrupt. I do beg your pardon.'

As the steward leaves you stare in shock. 'Viscount Sharp? Really?' you shout.

'Of course,' sneers Sharp triumphantly. 'Did you think I was a worthless commoner like you? I have a title, a *genuine* first-class ticket and in five minutes I shall be on a lifeboat and you, well... Let me tell you what I'm going to do,' he gloats. 'I will push you over the railings. Or stab you with my little knife here. Or knock you out with a single blow. Or simply choke you with my bare hands...'

BRIDGE (B) DECK

You don't doubt it. Sharp is clearly fit and stands with confidence. But you're sick of running. You square up to him. He seems surprised at your bravado.

'Such confidence from a weakling. Just like my worthless flower-loving friend. I shall enjoy this.'

You've been in a fight or two in your time and you know a lot of ways to counter the threats he has made. You just need to be sure you're in the right position to do them.

As Sharp makes each attack you must choose the correct counter-move. You cannot use a move that you are not in the correct position to begin.

1. PUSHING YOU OVER THE RAILING

Sharp rushes towards you with the clear intent of knocking you over the side into the freezing sea. As you stand before him, you know of four possible defenses:

A. DEFENSIVE CROUCH From a standing position you drop into a crouched position, lowering your centre of gravity and ensuring you cannot be pushed over.

B. PUSHING BACK From a standing position you push back on Sharp as he pushes you, resisting him and leaving you standing with your arms outstretched.

C. VAULT THE RAILING From a standing position you throw yourself over the railing before Sharp can even get to you, leaving you hanging from the railing over the sea.

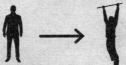

D. ANYTHING BUT THE FACE From a standing position, immediately form an X shape with your forearms in front of your face while shouting for mercy, leaving you standing with your arms crossed against your face.

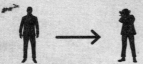

2. LUNGING AT YOU WITH HIS KNIFE

Unable to push you over, Sharp now jabs his gleaming knife at you. There are four counter moves:

A. KICK OUT From a crouching position you lash out with your leg unexpectedly, kicking his shin and causing him to drop the knife as he doubles over in pain, although you will immediately fall onto your back.

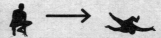

B. PASO DOBLE From any standing position you turn sideways like a bullfighter, allowing the knife to pass harmlessly across your body, leaving you standing sideways, hopefully unharmed.

C. DISARM HIM From a crouching position you surge upwards with your hands in a pincer shape, knocking the knife out of his grip with a sharp impact, leaving you standing with your arms outstretched.

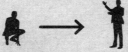

D. THE TIGER If you're standing with your arms crossed against your face you can drop forwards, throwing your arms out so that you are on all fours like a tiger, hopefully terrifying your foe – if they fear tigers.

3. PUNCHING YOUR LIGHTS OUT

Sharp now tries to knock you out with a haymaker punch.
There are four responses that you consider:

A. DUCK From any standing position, you bend quickly
forward so that his fist misses you entirely, before
shifting your legs so that you end in a stable crouching
position.

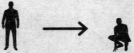

B. BLOCK While standing with your arms outstretched
you bring your arms up in front of your face, absorbing
and deflecting any blow with your forearms, ending in a
standing position with arms crossed against your face.

C. TAKE IT ON THE CHIN From any standing position,
remain in place and allow him to punch you, hoping that
his fist has been rendered weak by years of criminality.
The chances are high you will end up flat on your back.

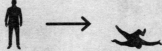

D. THE ARMADILLO If you are on all fours on the ground,
you can now ball yourself up into a crouching position to
possibly give yourself total protection. Or risk rolling
off the deck.

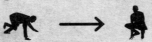

4. STRANGLING YOU

Finally, Sharp desperately resorts to choking the life out of you with his bare hands. Only four possibilities:

A. THROW HIM If you're standing with your arms stretched forward, you can grab his wrists to prevent his hands from even getting to your neck, then pull him backwards and fling him to the ground.

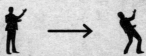

B. JACKET ATTACK If you are standing sideways you can swiftly remove your jacket and throw it at him before he sees it coming.

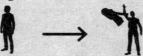

C. COUP DE GRÂCE If you're standing with your arms at your side, you think Sharp's anger will leave him vulnerable to a stout tap on the chin with your fist, sending him straight down to the floor.

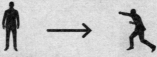

D. THE SPINNING TOP If you are in a crouched position you can attempt to begin spinning around and around on the spot like some kind of frenzied dervish. Perhaps it will confuse or stop him in some way. Although, to be honest, this has never actually worked...

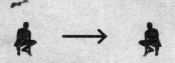

You must be able to get
through all the moves
in one go, or you
won't be able to defeat
Sharp and return to
the Grand Staircase.

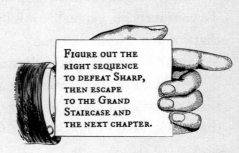

FIGURE OUT THE
RIGHT SEQUENCE
TO DEFEAT SHARP,
THEN ESCAPE
TO THE GRAND
STAIRCASE AND
THE NEXT CHAPTER.

CHAPTER EIGHT

PROMENADE (A) DECK

—— 29 ——

Solve the Artist's Riddle

The Grand Staircase is crowded with passengers desperately making their way upwards as the truth of the situation is setting in, but when you reach A Deck everyone suddenly stops.

You soon see the reason: a steward has positioned himself on the landing and holds a gun at the crowd. He fires the revolver in the air as a warning. 'Everybody stay back!' he shouts. 'The lifeboats are full! I've got five left in the chamber and I'm prepared to use them!'

'He's wrong about the boats,' says a man behind you. To your surprise you realize it is the tattooed horologist that you saved from the pool.

'I don't know why you're dressed like my artist friend,' he says, 'but I suspect it might be worth mentioning that he didn't just design my tattoos. He also designed that clock... and I helped him.' You see that behind the

steward is a highly ornate timepiece, carved with beautiful imagery of two recording angels and various other designs. 'The left one is Honour and the right is Glory,' he says. 'And I bet if we could get the clock to chime it would distract the steward long enough for someone to tackle him. But we'd need to use one of the master clocks to change it, and I don't know which one controls it. Arthur always said he didn't like to think any other clock could be the master of this one, so he kept it a secret,' he adds. 'That always struck me as an odd thing for him to say, but when I asked him about it, he simply scrawled some words on the back of this menu, which I held on to. You know, I think he may have done the art for this as well.'

ESCAPE THE TITANIC

He hands you the page from the menu. You notice that there are slices missing from each pie.

Main Course
Seafood Pies

Scallop Pie

Crab Pie

Eel Pie

Halibut Pie

On the back of the menu are the following strange words:

These lines, I write, but you must draw.

For the **first**, you must travel from Glory's empty hand to Honour's stylus.

Then to the point where their gazes meet, and end at 7.

For the **second**, you journey from the centre of the wreath to the centre of the world, then to Glory's empty hand.

Again to the point of their gazes' meeting and ending on Honour's stylus.

Once you know where the hands must be, it's easy as a certain pie to see.

The number of the master clock is in their quantity.

'Does this help?' asks the horologist. It does. By following the instructions you can find a pattern which will help you discover the number of the master clock. And it also explains why the clock has so many sea creatures on it.

FIND THE NUMBER
OF THE MASTER
CLOCK TO MOVE ON
TO CHALLENGE 30.

Rewire the Master Clock

The horologist leads you to the small nondescript room where the relevant master clock is housed. 'Once we change this, all the clocks connected to it will change, and then the Honour and Glory clock will chime.' In the distance you hear another gunshot, but thankfully no cries follow it, so you assume the steward was firing at the ceiling again.

'We must hurry,' he says quickly. He finds the master clock underneath a bank of dials showing the positions of all the clocks on the ship.

'But they're all different! Something has knocked all the clocks out of synchronization,' he mutters. 'I heard that some rats were running around in the electrical room, perhaps it was that.'

He finds the plan for an electrical circuit bypass. 'We'll need to find and chart the correct path that will only trigger the affected clocks.' He says.

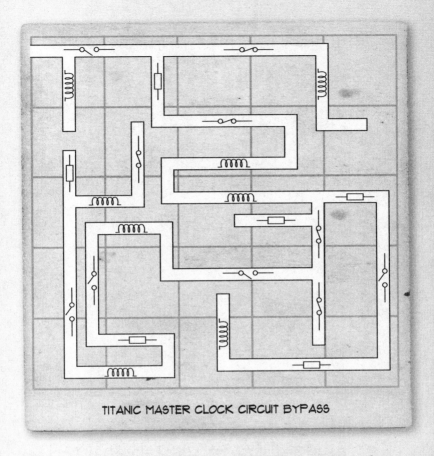

TITANIC MASTER CLOCK CIRCUIT BYPASS

There are some strips of paper with diagrams on, perhaps these can help you work out the way to go.

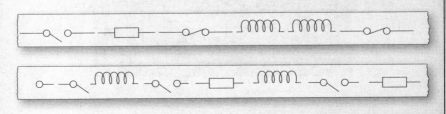

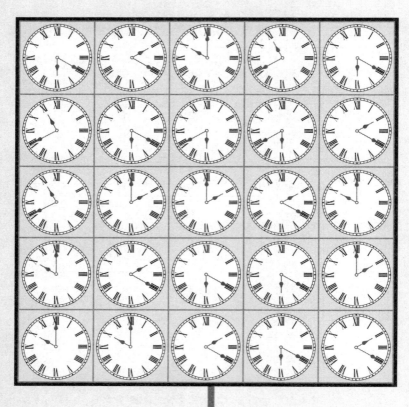

ESCAPE THE TITANIC

'And then what?' you ask frantically. He gestures to the wall of clock faces.

'Once we've figured out the path, we'll need to take note of the time shown by each clock on that path. If the circuit passes through a clock twice we will need to use that time twice.'

'Use it how?' you ask, as he flips through a pile of other documents and instructions.

'It seems the master clocks on this ship use something called the Beta Bee system to fix electrical errors.'

'... the what?'

'Apparently, the designer was a big fan of bees. And the Greek alphabet.'

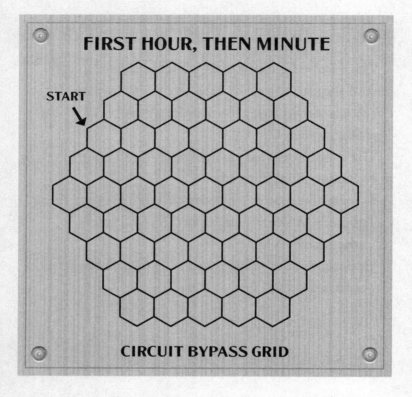

FIRST HOUR, THEN MINUTE

START

CIRCUIT BYPASS GRID

The horologist searches the many panels and switches on the wall until he finds a honeycomb-shaped grid with multiple slots.

'Ah! We have to put the correctly shaped bypass plate into this to resynchronize all the clocks.' He then opens a nearby box and pulls out four pieces of metal that look like Greek letters rendered from hexagons: the bypass plates. You peer at the shapes.

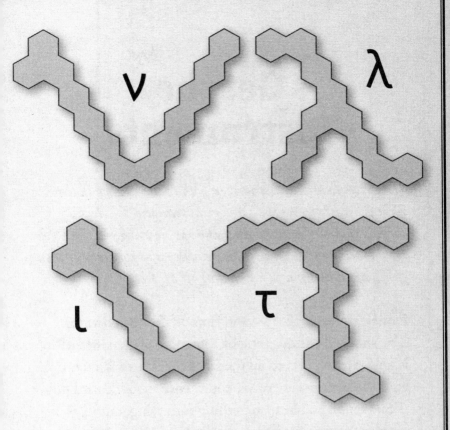

'So, we need to... find the right electrical path... then find the right clocks... then somehow use them to find out which of these shapes we need to place in the grid?'

'Yes!'

'Thank goodness – I was worried it would be complicated!'

ONCE YOU KNOW THE CORRECT BYPASS PLATE, YOU CAN SYNC UP THE CLOCKS AND MOVE ON TO CHALLENGE 31.

Get the Instruments

You activate the clock, and then both rush out back to the Grand Staircase. As the horologist predicted, the clock's chime is loud and distracting, and the steward swivels round, allowing several of the passengers at the front of the group to grab him and knock him off his feet.

Panicked, he breaks free and runs off down a corridor. The shocked passengers look uncertain about whether it is now safe to proceed up the staircase. There is a tense and fearful atmosphere as people worry about their fate.

Suddenly, you hear something surprising: music. Everyone turns to see that the on-board musicians have sat down and begun to play. Their beautiful melody is so surprising that the atmosphere begins to lighten...

But something is missing, and it's not quite working.

Some of the musicians aren't playing, merely standing among the crowd, and there is no piano. One of them makes his way over to you. He seems to recognize you from earlier. So much for this disguise!

'I'm Jock. I don't suppose you have a spare piano in your coat pocket, do you? Some of our instruments got a bit damaged on the way over.'

'What do you need?' you ask. Maybe if more of them are playing, the passengers will be calmer and it will be easier to make your way up those stairs.

'We need a cello, a violin and a double bass. Oh, and that piano I mentioned!'

'I have a piano,' exclaims a large-moustached gentleman nearby, 'in my cabin on this deck! You'll find it in B20.'

You turn and realize... it's William Bailey!

Before you can say anything, he leans forward and says, 'We'll talk in a moment. Help me get this piano.'

Jock explains that the other musicians also have spare instruments in their cabins. As it's very noisy, and they are too far away, you and William will have to fetch them yourselves. If only Jock could remember their cabin numbers...

'The violinist's cabin was definitely on the other side of the corridor,' he rambles, almost incoherently. 'I had to turn right out of my cabin to get to it. My cabin number, you ask? Um... well, I hung a tie on the door handle to help me find it. The double bass player was next door to me... can't remember which side. He kept complaining about the cellist being noisy, even though there were three cabins separating them and I couldn't hear the cellist... Oh, and I used to have to turn left to get to the violinist, but he changed rooms because he didn't like being opposite the double bass player. Ironically, he ended up being driven barmy by the piano playing in the adjoining room!'

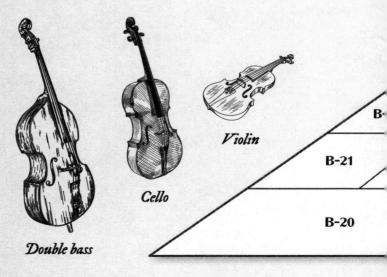

Violin

Cello

Double bass

B-

B-21

B-20

Together with William, you make your way to B20 and collect the piano. Its wheels are wobbly, but after 30 seconds you've managed to push it 15 feet. You need to find the other instruments. After pushing for 1 minute and 50 seconds, you notice the room to your left has a tie on its handle.

Which room has which instrument?

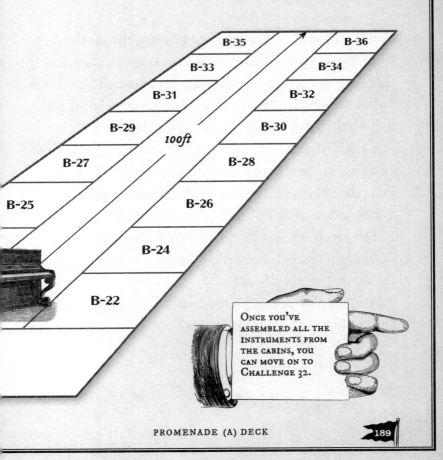

100ft

B-35   B-36
B-33   B-34
B-31   B-32
B-29   B-30
B-27   B-28
B-25   B-26
B-24
B-22

ONCE YOU'VE ASSEMBLED ALL THE INSTRUMENTS FROM THE CABINS, YOU CAN MOVE ON TO CHALLENGE 32.

Count the Bullets

You deliver the instruments to the grateful band, who immediately strike up 'Alexander's Ragtime Band', lifting the spirits of all present. The passengers begin moving up the stairs with more alacrity, and you go to join them, when William suddenly grabs your arm.

'Come with me!' When you knew him at the Harland & Wolff dockyards, William wore stained work clothes and his facial hair was unruly. Despite his trimmed beard and stylish suit and hat, it's clearly the same man. It's thanks to his help that you got this far, so you follow him.

'I know you must be confused. The truth is I was hired by a wealthy gentleman who intended to travel on the ship. He was concerned that his brother was going to try to rob and possibly kill him.'

'His brother being Viscount Sharp?' you say, as you follow him towards the parlour suites, the most luxurious accommodation on board.

'Yes, the Viscount is his brother. My employer, the Honourable Linnaeus Sharp, is also a dear friend of mine.

PROMENADE (A) DECK

'Viscount Sharp is particularly dangerous,' he continues, 'so to protect my employer I sought to alter the design of the very ship itself. This is why I worked alongside you at the docks, I was installing various secret devices, passageways and escape routes. Some of which you have yourself used, I understand.'

'And you encouraged me to be on board?' you ask.

'That's correct. I felt you had a great future. But I didn't anticipate that the ship would strike an iceberg...' he shakes his head, then looks determined.

'Now, let's retrieve Linnaeus Sharp, and get along to the lifeboats...'

But as you walk past a portrait hanging on some rather intricate wallpaper, you note that, strangely, someone seems to have put holes in the eyes. You point this out to William, and he in turn points across to a nearby porthole...

He examines the hole in the glass of the porthole with concern, but then you hear a cry from the nearby parlour. You both rush in to find the steward from earlier, holding a man, who you presume to be Linnaeus, at gunpoint.

ESCAPE THE TITANIC

'Stay back, both of you!' cries the steward. 'I have plenty of bullets and I'm not afraid to use them.'

'Even to shoot innocent people?' William asks, putting his hands in the air nonetheless.

'The viscount promised that I'd face no repercussions. And anyway, what's one more body at the bottom of the sea?' he snarls. He's clearly crazed and you know from your first two encounters with him that he's not shy of pulling the trigger. Impulsively, William darts forward. The steward pulls back the hammer on the gun.

You could dodge. Or you could throw yourself at him. Or you could heroically throw yourself in front of William. Thoughts go shooting through your brain: he hasn't reloaded. How many of the six bullets he had in his revolver are left?

ONCE YOU KNOW HOW MANY BULLETS THE STEWARD HAS LEFT YOU CAN ACT, AND HOPEFULLY MOVE UP TO THE BOAT DECK.

CHAPTER NINE

BOAT DECK

— 33 —

Send a Message

*You manage to rescue Linnaeus Sharp from the steward's
clutches. The steward runs off howling. The three of you
return to the stairs and carefully ascend to the final deck in
your journey: the Boat Deck. You felt like you would never
get here.*

In the darkness all is a mixture of order and chaos.
Stewards and other members of the crew are guiding
passengers to the lifeboats, a few of which seem to have
been launched already.

   You look to Linnaeus and William, only to see they
have already walked off and are assisting with the loading
of the boats. You assumed they had a lifeboat already
waiting, but you realize now that perhaps all they ever
planned was to give help to the women and children who
are first in line. William Bailey returns.

'I know you want to get off the ship. And perhaps that will be possible. But I still need your help.'

Before you can ask any further questions, William is suddenly introducing you to a man that you realize with shock is the ship's captain. The next moment William seems to have disappeared again and the captain, his face a mix of horror and determination, has a task for you.

ESCAPE THE TITANIC

'I've been reliably informed you know semaphore. We're short-handed and it's chaos here on deck as we try to get the women and children into the boats, and... I've only just learned our telegraph operators sent the wrong position to any possible rescuing vessels.'

He sighs deeply, then continues.

'Officer Boxhall is calculating our true position at the other end of the deck, and intends to use semaphore to signal it. Will you stand outside the Marconi Room and ensure he relays it to them as soon as you see it?' You have no choice but to acquiesce as you can tell your chances of getting on a lifeboat at the moment are slim, and perhaps helping the captain will increase your chances.

You go to stand by the Marconi Room, where the telegraph operators work. Shortly you see a man, who must be Officer Boxhall, waving two semaphore flags. Remembering the semaphore system, you quickly note down the numbers, although it is rather hard to see them in the dark.

Suddenly, a huge gust of wind, combined with a lurch of the ship, causes Boxhall to lose both flags. He was only four digits from the end!

Linnaeus and William are standing nearby, and after speaking to Boxhall briefly they grab two translucent blankets that some people brought onto deck to try and stay warm and begin waving them around in front of one of the funnels.

The shapes they are making almost look like semaphore, except you don't recognize the symbols. Perhaps they are confused.

You wave and shrug at them, and they talk briefly, before pointing at you and then simultaneously turning their heads to their left about 45 degrees.

At first you have no idea what this means, but then suddenly you realize, and you are able to decode the last four numbers relating to the ship's position.

CALCULATE THE LAST FOUR DIGITS OF THE SHIP'S POSITION TO MOVE ON TO CHALLENGE 34.

34

Outsmart Sharp

The captain seems pleased with your help, but has much to do, so he marches off. Just as you are about to walk away you feel a tap on your shoulder. You know who it is going to be before you even turn around: Sharp.

You have no fear of him anymore. And he has no false bonhomie left either. His face is a mask of hatred.

'Stowaway!' he hisses. A couple of able seamen come over, accompanied by a man who you suspect may be the master-at-arms. Sharp tells them, 'This... person is a stowaway. A parasite nestled in the ship's bosom. And not only that, but a murderer, killer of Mr. Demone!' The crew members glare at you. The master-at-arms narrows his eyes. 'Yes, I have heard about a stowaway.' He points a finger at you... 'I have heard about a stowaway who is a brave individual who has helped and saved many aboard this vessel.' He turns to point and stare at Sharp. 'And I have heard from reliable sources that it was in fact a first-class passenger who killed Demone – a viscount.'

BOAT DECK

You are amazed when, as if like magic, Sharp's demeanour immediately transforms.

'Oh lor' guvnor, I never meant to be no hero,' he says in a thick cockney accent. 'I just did what me heart told me. Then the viscount threatened me, told me to off Mr. Demone or I'd get a sharp thing in me guttyworks! Made me swap clothes with 'im, pretend to be a toff...'

Sharp prostrates himself, wringing his hands. 'But I couldn't do it. When I saw him just now I thought the only way I could get you to listen was to pretend to be 'im. I'm most terribly sorry, I am.'

Somehow his bluff is working, and Sharp's hammy performance seems to be resonating. You consider pleading as well, but you know you couldn't match his grovelling. The master-at-arms is still slightly sceptical so he turns to Sharp and subjects him to a series of questions about his on-board activities.

As Sharp answers, you notice inconsistencies in his account. If you can point these out to the master-at-arms, maybe you can prove your identity.

MAA: I hear you rescued a tattooed gentleman from drowning in a mineral bath?

Sharp: No, it was a swimming pool. He must have hit his head on the diving board. It's lucky he didn't get electrocuted by the loose wire!

a) It was a mineral bath.
b) There was no diving board.
c) There was no loose wire.

MAA: You assisted Mycroft Finsdale and Clemmie Nithercott when she broke her leg?

Sharp: I did. We found out he was very ill so they decided to stay in the library together.

a) Their surnames are the wrong way round.
b) She broke her arm.
c) They didn't stay in the library.

MAA: You generously helped a third-class passenger by giving him a haircut so he could move on through the ship...

Sharp: No, it was because he had two first-class tickets. I gave him the Hooray Henry haircut. Maybe they would have been more convinced by the Hello George, as that was the second fastest haircut.

a) The third-class passenger did not have tickets.
b) You did not give him the Hooray Henry.
c) The Hello George is not the second fastest.

MAA: And you didn't steal Linnaeus Sharp's bag from the luggage compartment?

Sharp: Well, I accidentally helped this person do it but I realized my mistake later. The bag belongs to a healer who uses plants such as Dionaea muscipula.

a) You stole the bag from his room.
b) He said it was his brother's bag.
c) Dionaea muscipula is not a healing plant.

MAA: In fact, didn't you rescue this very man from being handcuffed to a bunk?

Sharp: I did, sir!

MAA: Then this question is key: if A+B=D, what does C+E equal?

a) A
b) D
c) B

CORRECT SHARP'S ANSWERS TO PROVE YOU ARE THE STOWAWAY AND MOVE TO CHALLENGE 35.

35

Open the Watch

The master-at-arms seems satisfied that you are the real stowaway. Sharp's face transforms once again to his original aristocratic sneer as he spots something over their shoulder. 'Ah, providence. Toodle-oo!' With the delicate swiftness of a ballerina he sidesteps all of you and in an instant has his knife tight against his brother's neck.

'Lovely to see you again, Weevil,' he spits, 'and we're in just the right spot.' They're standing by the mast for the crow's nest and he indicates for his brother to begin climbing, followed by him. 'You had better come too, stowaway,' he hisses.

You turn to the seamen and master-at-arms. The boat is creaking alarmingly and passengers are panicking. 'I'll deal with this. Keep loading the boats,' you say.

BOAT DECK

By the time you're at the top, Sharp, still holding his brother at knife-point, has used the key he stole from Demone to open a box. 'This is normally where they keep the binoculars,' he says with a nasty smile. 'Instead, there is this.'

He shows you an incredibly ornate pocket watch. It's elliptical, similar to an egg.

'Finally – it's mine!' he says with manic glee. 'The *Titanic* Egg. How do you open it?' he asks his brother.

'I have no idea,' says Linnaeus.

'Don't be absurd!' Sharp barks furiously. 'You're the one who had it crafted.'

'Actually it's a gift from Alexander Cronos, a horologist friend,' he tells you.

'The tattooed man?' you ask. He smiles. 'Of course, you saved his life. Yes, he made this for me as a present for all the work I gave him. He made the timepieces for all my conservatories across the continent. Stockholm, Edinburgh, Prague...'

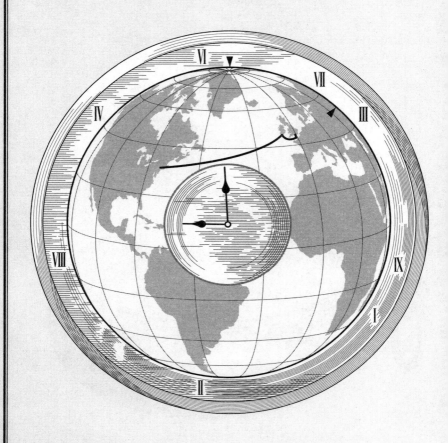

'Shut up!' Sharp shouts. 'You always get everything! Well not this time – this is mine.' He peers at the watch's face, trying to pry it open.

'What do you mean?' says Linnaeus, confused. 'You're the eldest, you inherited the title, the estate, all the money...' Sharp points his dagger accusingly.

'None of that mattered. You were still the favourite. Going for walks on the estate with father. And then I get saddled with a crumbling old mansion and barely enough money to survive while you make thousands selling flowers to idiots.'

'You gambled the money away. And it's not just flowers, my arboretums—'

'Quiet!' Sharp cuts him off. 'Then I hear you're going to sail on this new ship they're building, the *Titanic*, and your friend is making you a special watch, a replica of some old German gewgaw from 400 years ago! And locked inside is your "most precious possession" they said. I knew then I had to have that. It has to be an enormous diamond, or some rare artifact that will sell for millions.' Sharp throws the watch to you casually.

'OK puzzler. There's a secret compartment. Open it and I'll share the contents with you. Fail and I'll gut both you and my brother in a flash.'

He points at the image of the globe on the dial, which you realize has a small line on it that indicates the intended journey of *Titanic* across the Atlantic, including the first departure and final arrival points.

'You can rotate the globe dial face,' he says. You do so, noticing as it clicks smoothly around, while the hands at the centre stay immobile, as do the Roman numerals on the surrounding ring.

'All Alexander Cronos ever told me about it was: "The watch will open when I press on the marked location. The departure and arrival should be on my hands. And as above, so below."'

This suggests that you need to check the bottom of the watch. You turn it over to find more movable rings with strange arrows, the cardinal directions and some odd symbols. You find that the top ring of symbols can be turned but the central ring and the outer one with the directions stays static too. This is your greatest challenge so far. You need to work out which direction to turn the globe and by how much. You look questioningly at Linnaeus.

'The Latin text reads "Depart on the minute. Arrive on the hour.",' he explains. You quickly work out how far you need to turn the watch and realise that the bottom half must be the same. What this reveals will help you deduce the location you need to press on the globe.

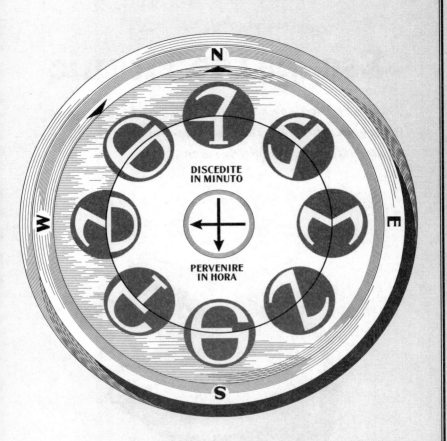

DISCEDITE
IN MINUTO

PERVENIRE
IN HORA

ONCE YOU KNOW
WHERE TO PRESS ON
THE WATCH, MOVE
ONTO THE FINAL
CHALLENGE...

36

Escape the Titanic

*You press the location and a tiny button clicks. The watch
snaps open... Both you and Sharp lean forward to see...
an acorn. Sharp is completely stunned.*

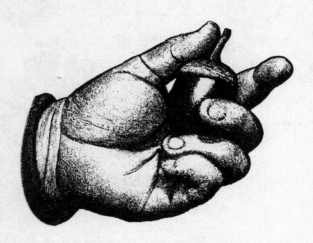

'An acorn... An acorn? Wait... it must be a gem, disguised! Or it contains a clue to a treasure's location,' he gabbles. Linnaeus smiles wryly and shakes his head. 'No brother, just an acorn. When I was six, I walked with father in the woods near our estate. He picked up the acorn and told me about the trees, how they grow from tiny seeds but become immense and then get made into houses, carriages, even the tops of masts on great ships like this. It's what started me on my path through life.' Sharp is shaking his head frantically in disbelief. 'No, no!'

'It's true. He tried to give you one, once. You threw it at the dog.' Sharp's face is pale.

'But I spent so much time planning how to get this... Months and months bribing officials and making alliances with gangsters! They betrayed me, tied me to a bed, I escaped and made my way here... for an acorn?'

ESCAPE THE TITANIC

Linnaeus picks up the acorn. 'We all choose how we spend our time,' he says gently. 'It's timepieces like this that enabled people to travel across the oceans. And here, on this ship, our time is running out. Why don't we go back down to the deck?'

'You first!', howls Sharp, and he leaps forward, aiming to push his brother from the crow's nest. But intuitively you pull him out of the way. Missing his target and losing his footing, Sharp sails over the edge, clean out of the nest. You both lean over and see Sharp plummet all the way down and off the side of the boat into the dark depths of the sea. You both solemnly climb down the ladder to the deck. Linnaeus looks extremely sad.

'He was a vicious man but he was my brother. Thank you for your help.' He puts the acorn back in the watch and snaps it shut. 'Now let's get to a boat.'

You find William Bailey nearby, organizing the boarding. After hearing about Sharp he nods soberly. 'Sad, but inevitable. Well then, I know that Linnaeus and I both plan to remain on board to the bitter end. But for you, I recommend boat 18.'

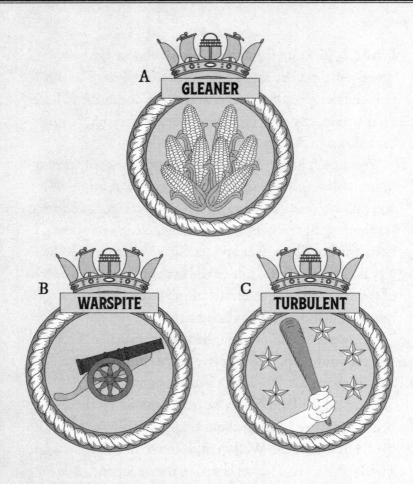

You decide to take his advice and find lifeboat number 18. The sailors seem to have written an unofficial tally of which boats are still aboard and where they are, but when you look at it you realize they haven't written any numbers, only symbols.

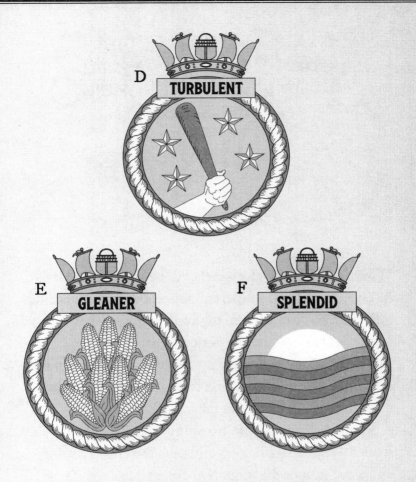

You desperately ask a harried-looking sailor what the symbols mean. 'It was a sort of game during lifeboat drills. We used badges from ships we'd been on instead of numbers. I can't remember how it worked though. Wait, I know that A, over there, is Boat 8. I hope that helps.'

G **TURBULENT**

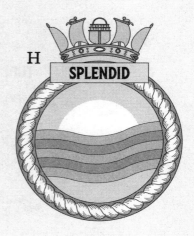

H **SPLENDID**

'There's something else which will help you figure it out,' he says, pointing to a different noticeboard, and he rushes off before you can get him to simply tell you what the numbers are. You find the noticeboard. It seems to have some kind of mathematical puzzle on it, with the symbols in various places. You can use this to help you work out the different values and thereby which boat is which.

All around you people are piling into lifeboats, stewards trying to fill them and keep men from getting on before women and children. You can feel the deck beginning to tilt drastically backwards. You run frantically to lifeboat 18 and arrive to find that it's almost full, but there is no one else waiting for it and there is one final space... But then you see a woman – tired and desperate – carrying a small baby, struggling against the wind. The decision is surprisingly easy for you.

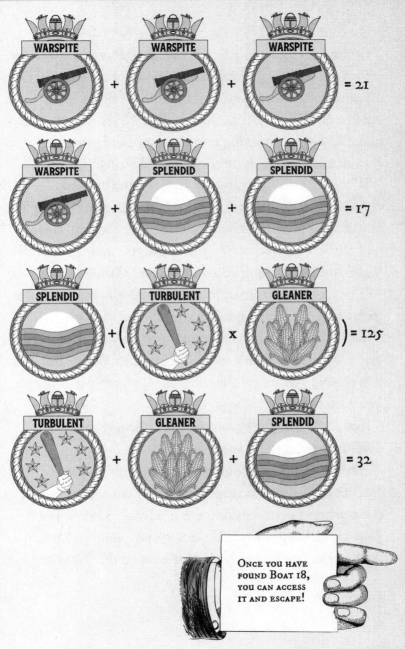

WARSPITE + WARSPITE + WARSPITE = 21

WARSPITE + SPLENDID + SPLENDID = 17

SPLENDID + (TURBULENT x GLEANER) = 125

TURBULENT + GLEANER + SPLENDID = 32

ONCE YOU HAVE FOUND BOAT 18, YOU CAN ACCESS IT AND ESCAPE!

You run over and guide her to the lifeboat, and help lower it into the water. Looking around you can see that almost all of the others are gone and a couple of fights have broken out on deck. The deck is tilting back even further and the ship is beginning to make very loud groaning, creaking noises and is physically shuddering. This is it.

The ship breaks up around you, splintering and collapsing under its own weight. It seems to be tipping up and tearing itself in half at the same time. Seconds before you are thrown backwards you think you spot the face of William Bailey giving you one last rueful smile.

The ice-cold water knocks the air out of your lungs – it feels like you are being hit by a train. You struggle to stay afloat. And you know that even if you do you will surely die of hypothermia in a matter of minutes. But just as you're going down for the third time, a hand pulls you up into a lifeboat.

You look up into the face of your rescuer... and you don't recognize them at all.

But that is how it should be. You weren't rescued because of some great achievement or status. You were rescued because of the common kindness of humanity. This great disaster has taken a huge toll, but, with much skill, perseverance and luck, you escaped the *Titanic*.

The End

BOAT DECK

Afterword

None of the scenarios depicted in this book are intended to be true or accurate portrayals of the tragic events that took place on RMS *Titanic* on the night of 14 April 1912. They have been invented to challenge or entertain the

reader, and are not to be taken as fact or as a reflection on any of the real people involved. The genuine bravery and heroism of those who both survived and died stands as an inspiration for everyone.

Hints

1 READ THE DECK PLAN

Third-Class hint: A letter and a number can be found in the newspaper article.
Second-Class hint: William Bailey says that the 'A' Deck is a '12' for him.
First-Class hint: If A=12, you can shift all the letters by that amount.

2 ESCAPE THE CARGO HOLD

Third-Class hint: Only one of the crates' weights ends in a 3.
Second-Class hint: The box that needs lifting contains Champagne.
First-Class hint: One of the possible useful boxes is sadly inaccessible.

3 VENT THE BOILERS

Third-Class hint: Each stoker has a quality that makes them uniquely suited to use a particular valve.
Second-Class hint: Working out which stoker goes where gives you a five-letter code.
First-Class hint: Combine the correct pipe with the two-digit stoker order number.

4 FOLLOW THE RAT

Third-Class hint: The grid doesn't relate to the floor plan, but to the three lists of co-ordinates.
Second-Class hint: The co-ordinates create images that each give you a direction.
First-Class hint: The rats will turn left, right or go straight on in relation to their own orientation.

5 RESCUE SHARP

Third-Class hint: Sharp's directions are the reverse of what you want.
Second-Class hint: Only one of the bunks can be reached using Sharp's directions.
First-Class hint: The directions describe a cross-shaped path in the larger part of the room.

6 FIND THE RIGHT BAG

Third-Class hint: Sharp's brother is not a gardener.
Second-Class hint: The Physic Garden is frequented by the medical profession.
First-Class hint: One of the symbols relates to Sharp's brother's true profession.

7 FIND THE RIGHT PIGEONHOLE

Third-Class hint: There's a clue in the postmark.
Second-Class hint: The numbers on the postcode supply a route.
First-Class hint: The postmark also gives the final direction.

8 GET THROUGH THE GATE

Third-Class hint: Take a deep breath and look carefully.
Second-Class hint: The bubble path passes through 'Halve' once.
First-Class hint: Look out for extra portholes, gulls and steam, to name three.

9 FIND THE RIGHT DOOR

Third-Class hint: If two are telling the truth, the other three are lying.

Second-Class hint: They know the truth, but the numbers are floating.

First-Class hint: The doors are numbered 11–15.

10 SAVE THE DROWNING MAN

Third-Class hint: You will need to take a long route.

Second-Class hint: The line from the man to the towel is the shortest.

First-Class hint: The life-ring line must go under the towel line but over the switch line.

11 GET A CLUE FROM HIS TATTOOS

Third-Class hint: He's a superstitious soul.

Second-Class hint: He doesn't want to see the sea.

First-Class hint: Look at the number of this challenge.

12 OPEN THE HATCH

Third-Class hint: The shape of the compass is similar to your escape route.

Second-Class hint: Actual times are less important than their relative directions.

First-Class hint: West is clockwise and east is anticlockwise.

13 GIVE HIM A HAIRCUT

Third-Class hint: Shave time off using the clippers.

Second-Class hint: Start by working out how long 'The Baron' takes.

First-Class hint: Of the two quickest styles, only one will allow him to blend into the crowd.

14 STAY OUT OF THE LIGHT

Third-Class hint: There is only one safe route.

Second-Class hint: If your feet get wet, take two steps on the spot.

First-Class hint: Right is the right direction.

15 FIND THE RIGHT TUNE

Third-Class hint: Look for repeated notes.

Second-Class hint: It's not a French title.

First-Class hint: The note F refers to the letter E.

16 ANSWER HIS QUESTIONS

Third-Class hint: The answers are hiding in plain sight.

Second-Class hint: Port is on the left.

First-Class hint: Sharp never told you his full name.

17 MIX A COCKTAIL

Third-Class hint: Each symbol has three different elements.

Second-Class hint: Work out which ingredients you don't have.

First-Class hint: The symbols indicate the bottle colour, shape, and label.

18 TURN THE TABLES

Third-Class hint: The first nonogram gives you the missing part of the second.

Second-Class hint: The first nonogram is asymmetrical.

First-Class hint: The second nonogram shows you where you are.

19 FIND A FRIEND
Third-Class hint: The two letters are dated two days apart, but both are Mondays.
Second-Class hint: Construction generally comes before launch.
First-Class hint: Haircuts usually make hair shorter.

20 HELP THE DOCTOR
Third-Class hint: You have seen numbers like these before.
Second-Class hint: Look at the objects the people are holding.
First-Class hint: You can only get past people who are smiling.

21 GET HER TO THE ROOM
Third-Class hint: By comparing weights, you can work out the cutlery weight of everything.
Second-Class hint: If four sets of cutlery = two silver bowls, then four sets of cutlery = one candelabra.
First-Class hint: Try adding all the items up and halving the result to give you the answer.

22 FIND HIS FILE
Third-Class hint: Note how many rows and columns of drawers there are.
Second-Class hint: Each suit has ten number cards and three face cards.
First-Class hint: Put the suits in alphabetical order.

23 OPEN THE BOX
Third-Class hint: Two of the masks could be read upside-down.
Second-Class hint: Look at the number of lines in each rune.

24 SOLVE THE MYSTERY
Third-Class hint: The myroglyphic heads are looking in different directions.
Second-Class hint: Some of the lines on the books form a path.
First-Class hint: Myron's note will tell you which lines to follow.

First-Class hint: Pay close attention to which eye and which tooth was lost in order to identify the brothers.

25 DISGUISE YOURSELF
Third-Class hint: The items in the painting are positioned in a way that matches the room.
Second-Class hint: The thing on the floor is a covering, but not a rug.
First-Class hint: Hold the page up to the light to see how things line up.

26 FIND THE ERRORS
Third-Class hint: Take a closer look at Poseidon's fork.
Second-Class hint: The Vitruvian Man is missing some limbs.
First-Class hint: The four errors make a set that you might find on a table.

27 DECODE THE MESSAGE
Third-Class hint: The key provides a clue.
Second-Class hint: 2 is a prime number.
First-Class hint: 89 is the 24th prime number.

28 FIGHT SHARP
Third-Class hint: You can't fight if you're lying on your back.

Second-Class hint: Moves that start from a standing position are very helpful.
First-Class hint: Your final move is appropriately named.

29 FIND THE ANSWER

Third-Class hint: Draw lines between the places mentioned.
Second-Class hint: Clocks have hands.
First-Class hint: The slices of the seafood pies might resemble something else.

30 CHOOSE THE METAL PLATE

Third-Class hint: The circuit order is at the bottom of the page.
Second-Class hint: The clock hands will give you the directions.
First-Class hint: Draw one line for the hour hand, another for the minute, and keep going.

31 GET THE INSTRUMENTS

Third-Class hint: If it takes 30 seconds for the piano to move 15 feet, where is it after 110 seconds?
Second-Class hint: Which rooms would you hear the piano playing from?
First-Class hint: The violinist's cabin can only be in one particular half of the corridor.

32 COUNT THE BULLETS

Third-Class hint: He's two shots down before you've even reached this challenge.
Second-Class hint: Both pictures include bullet holes.
First-Class hint: Take a good look at the wallpaper pattern.

33 SEND A MESSAGE

Third-Class hint: Look at the flag patterns and the square patterns.
Second-Class hint: It helps to tilt your head.
First-Class hint: Three of them are divisible.

34 OUTSMART SHARP

Third-Class hint: All the answers are in Chapter Two.
Second-Class hint: Professor Myron Nithercott.
First-Class hint: The key's shapes are key.

35 OPEN THE WATCH

Third-Class hint: How much must you turn the globe, and which way?
Second-Class hint: Turn the top symbols the same amount to form numbers.
First-Class hint: Connect the numbers to find that X marks the spot.

36 ESCAPE THE TITANIC

Third-Class hint: All the boat symbols are subtly different.
Second-Class hint: Look very closely before you do the sums.
First-Class hint: One wheat stalk is worth 1.

Solutions

1 READ THE DECK PLAN

You need a code key to know how to shift the code wheel. In the newspaper article Bailey gave you it says that 'Mr. Bailey even said that if he had to give the Titanic's A-Deck a rating between 1 to 10, he would give it a 12!' This indicates that in the code A=12, and employing that shift to the wheel gives you the following: A=12, B=13, C=14 etc. This translates the encoded numbers on the map into the deck names: 23/20/17/16/13/0/12/5/4 = LIFEBOATS; 24/16/16/5 24/16 19/16/3/16 = MEET ME HERE; 13/3/20/15/18/16 = BRIDGE; 4/19/16/23/5/16/3 = SHELTER; 4/12/23/0/0/25 = SALOON; 6/1/1/16/3 = UPPER; 24/20/15/15/23/16 = MIDDLE; 23/0/8/16/3 = LOWER; 0/3/23/0/1 = ORLOP.

2 ESCAPE THE CARGO HOLD

With the numbers on the manifest and the logical process of elimination you can establish the weights of the crates. The bottom-middle crate is labelled 40.0. The centre right crate ends in a 3, so must be 7.3, so the middle-left crate must be 7.0. The middle-centre crate ends in 0.0, so must be 10.0. The top-left crate must be 10.5. The top-middle crate must be 30.5. That means the bottom-left crate must be 33.5. The top-right crate must therefore be 13.5. The two possibilities for the bottom-right crate are 23.0 or 5.0. Since the crate that has to be lifted out of the way is heavier than you can lift, it must be the crate of Champagne, at 23.0 kg, so that leaves the bottom right as 5.0

10.5	30.5	13.5
7.0	10.0	7.3
33.5	40.0	5.0

You will need two crates to counterbalance the 23.0kg crate of Champagne. You options are the 13.5kg crate of Medical Supplies + either the 10.5 kg crate of Canned Soup or the 10.0 kg crate of Soap. However, the crate of Soap is underneath the 30.5 kg crate of Nuts and Bolts, which you are unable to lift. You will need the Medical Supplies and the Canned Soup.

3 VENT THE BOILERS

You need to learn two things: the correct pipe for the Aft Funnel and which stoker to put on which valve. Tracing all the pipes shows that pipe B leads to the Aft Funnel. Assign the stokers based on their personal expertise. Callum is very careful, so he'll work on the Air Pump; Thomas is tall so he can provide leverage for the Throttle Valve; Ernest is educated so can use the complicated Thrust Block; Simon is strong and dedicated so can stay on the Stop Valve; Albert has hearing problems so he can bear being on the High-Pressure Cylinder. On the manual are letter codes that give you two-digit numbers based on the order of the stoker's initials. CTESA=89. Combining these two details gives you *B89*, which can be found on the gauge, therefore venting the boilers through the Aft Funnel.

4 FOLLOW THE RAT

You need to learn which of the roman numerals indicates that the rat goes left, right or straight on. There are three in the electrical room at the beginning showing the respective Roman numerals, followed by a series of letter and number combinations. The piece of paper with a grid on it has a letter axis and a number axis. If you draw lines of movement based on the coordinates you are given, you get the following images.

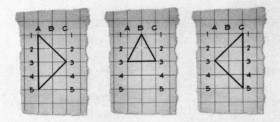

These arrow show you that I = right;
II = straight on; III = left

Using this as a guide, you can track the rats' paths. Remember that any turns are from the rat's point of view, so when it turns its orientation changes. The piebald rat turns round and goes out of the room the wrong way; the black rat simply runs into the wall; the white rat successfully gets to the exit.

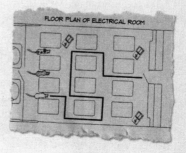

FLOOR PLAN OF ELECTRICAL ROOM

5 RESCUE SHARP

Follow Sharp's precise directions in reverse and trace them on the plan of the bunk room. Only one of the bunks could be reached in this way: 13. The shape it gives you will give the shape of the key needed to release him from the manacles. The key is D.

6 FIND THE RIGHT BAG

Sharp's brother is evidently a botanist, but particularly a medical one, because his picture shows him with plants that the leaflet tells us are medicinal. Therefore, the most likely label for his bag is a caduceus, a medical symbol.

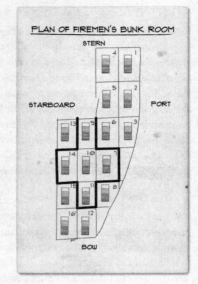

7 FIND THE KEY IN THE PIGEONHOLE

The letter that the postman hands you has three major clues to finding the key to the post room door: 1) The postcode numbers are the outline to the path which will take you to the hole that has the key. 2) The postmark grid shows where you begin, at the top right corner of Box D. Apply the numbers in the sequence on the letter as the illustration which will take you to Box K. 3) The compass on the watermark gives you an extra directional arrow to the exact location of the key.

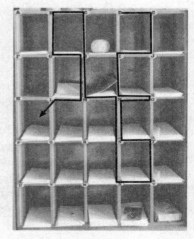

8 GET THROUGH THE GATE

By tracing this path through the numbers, you can take on 120 seconds to stay under water and examine the panels on the gate. The two identical panels are the second row on the right and the bottom row on the left. These are the ones that Sharp pressed on to release the gate.

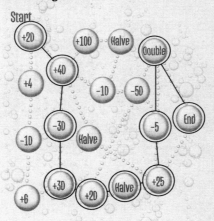

9 FIND THE RIGHT DOOR

There are only two people who could possibly be telling the truth because otherwise there are logical flaws in what they say. Callum Blackstaff thinks Poole is a liar so it can't be them together, and as Cloutier and Palmer think Poole's telling the truth it can't be either of them with Blackstaff either, so if Blackstaff is telling the truth then so must Francis McGillvray. Poole doesn't trust anyone else but Cloutier but if they're the truth-tellers then Palmer's statement on Poole's trustworthiness is wrong. Palmer now obviously can't be matched with anyone. McGillvray mistrusts the baker and is mistrusted by everyone else except Blackstaff. So the two truthtellers must be Blackstaff and McGillvray.

Which of them has the fastest route? They both do, but neither of them realize it. It is illogical that the Roman numerals would go X, XI, XII, XI, X because that would be 10, 11, 12, 15, 10. The wooden pieces in the water must be the missing numerals from the doors. As Door D has a V on it and a gap it can only be XIV, meaning the other doors are XI, XII, XIII and XV, i.e. 10, 11, 12, 13 and 14. As Door E looks like an X then it's clear Blackstaff saw it as X but McGillvray would have seen it marked as XV on the plans. Therefore, the correct door is Door E.

10 SAVE THE DROWNING MAN

The objects you need can be connected using the following lines without crossing.

11 GET A CLUE FROM HIS TATTOOS

Work out which clue is most likely to apply and use them to eliminate cabins until you are left with a single possibility. 1) Purity or knowing his surname wouldn't help with working out the cabin, so it is more likely he likes odd numbers. 2) Based on the first tattoo it seems likely he must dislike even numbers and so you can eliminate any even numbered cabins. 3) Being afraid of skeletons or liking the picture doesn't help at all but if he gets sea sick he won't be in a cabin with a window, eliminating 1, 3, 5 and 7, and leaving 9, 11 and 13. 4) No hat or urn is visible, so we can eliminate Cabin 9 based on his possible dislike of the number. 5) These symbols imply he is superstitious and therefore unlikely to stay in Cabin 13. So the man has Cabin 11.

12 OPEN THE HATCH

Find out two things: which way to turn each of the three handles, and how many times. 1) The compass on the map is shaped like a tilted square with an arrow marking at the top. The hatch is also square with the three handles in the corners, and the top left handle has a similar arrow shape, indicating that you need to think of those handles as being North, East and West. 2) From his journal you can determine: North London = 4; East Cape Town = 5 and West Santiago = 3. 3) The clocks for London and Cape Town are ahead of the Titanic's time (clockwise or forwards), and the clock for Santiago is behind (anti-clockwise or backwards).

4) This indicates that you need to turn the North handle right four times, the East handle right five times and the West handle left three times.

13 GIVE HIM A HAIRCUT

1) The Baron takes twice as long as it does to sterilize equipment and you can see in the image that it takes 2 minutes to sterilize a comb, so it takes 4 minutes, or 3 minutes 30 seconds with the clippers and brilliantine. 2) The Clockwise parting takes one and a half times the length of 'the most aristocratic haircut' (The Baron), so it takes six minutes, or six minutes twenty seconds with the macassar. 3) The Peacock is twice as quick as the haircut with the most timely name (The Clockwise), so it takes 3 minutes, or 2 minutes 20 seconds with the clippers and brilliantine. 4) The Basic Caruso takes three times the length of The Peacock using the clippers, so it takes 9 minutes 20 seconds with the brilliantine. 5) The Hooray Henry is three times faster than the haircut with the celebrity name (The Basic Caruso) so it takes 3 minutes, or 2 minutes 20 seconds with the clippers and brilliantine. 6) The Continental is as long as the other two shortest haircuts so it must be 3 minutes, but you cannot use the clippers. 7) The Hello George takes five times the length of the most international haircut (The Continental) so it takes 15 minutes 20 seconds with the brilliantine. 8) The Dapper David is one third quicker than the haircut that takes the longest (The Hello George) so it takes 10 minutes or 9 minutes 30 seconds with the clippers and the Macassar. This leaves us with both The Peacock and the Hooray Henry at 2 minutes 20 seconds. However, you must remember the other objective is that the haircut will enable him to blend into the crowd, and The Peacock will definitely not allow that. So the fastest and best haircut is The Hooray Henry.

14 STAY OUT OF THE LIGHT

Route C is your only possible route of escape.

15 FIND THE RIGHT TUNE

You must find which song's title is hidden in the coded notes. 1) The note sequence is A, F, D#, B, F, B, G#, C#, F#, A#, E, C, A#, C. If the song were 'Valse Septembre' then the note F would denote the letter A, but F is repeated two letters later where E would be, and therefore it can't be that. If the song were 'Maple Leaf Rag' then we would expect to see two notes repeating, denoting the letters '...le le...'. Only 'Nearer My God to Thee' follows the correct code sequence with F=E at both the second and fifth position.

16 ANSWER THE QUESTIONS

1. A (mentioned in the Introduction).
2. A (you were there at the time).
3. C (this was where you stowed away).
4. C (not a trick question).
5. A
6. C
7. A
8. C (you don't know his surname).
9. C (you might be the 3,122nd person on board).

17 MIX A COCKTAIL

The only drink that does not require fruit or vegetable garnishes is the Tuxedo. You know the symbols for the lemon juice and the angostura bitters, so you can use the process of elimination and comparison to work out that each symbol denotes the bottle shape, label shape and bottle colour.

For the Tuxedo you'll need bottles of maraschino, absinthe, orange bitters, gin and dry vermouth.

18 TURN THE TABLES

To calculate where the tables are, you must cross-reference how many rectangles must be filled in each line. The first nonogram reveals the number 9, which is the missing number in the second nonogram.

Once you add 9 to the missing line you can complete the nonogram table plan, which clearly commemorates the ship's maiden voyage.

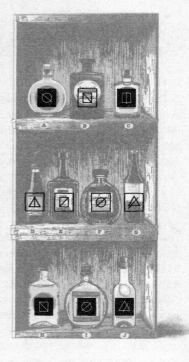

Bottle shapes

Rounded   Square   Classic wine bottle style

Bottle labels

Square   Rounded   Rounded top square bottom

Bottle colour

Clear   Tinted

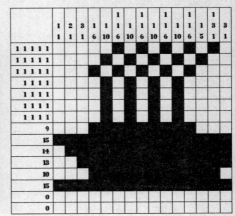

19 FIND A FRIEND

Although the letters were sent on consecutive dates, they are both Monday, indicating that the dates are not in the same year. The second letter refers to Titanic being under construction while the first says he is going to embark on it, so the first letter is the more recent. In the other letter, Vivian refers wearing glasses so anyone not wearing glasses can be eliminated.

The same letter refers to bowler hats and bow ties but doesn't say that Vivian wears them. And while they state that they have long hair, the later letter changes that. The chronologically second letter says Vivian wears a hat and has short hair and will not be smiling. It also states that Vivian has extreme hay fever, eliminating anyone wearing a flower. The only person matching this description is 13.

20 HELP THE DOCTOR

In the previous challenge, some of the thirty people are smiling and some are not. You will also notice: 2 is wearing a scarf, that can be used to support the splint; 4 has some water, to bathe the wound; 12 has some alcohol, for pain relief; 24 has a stick to use as a splint. Therefore, this is the best possible path, where you can pass every number you need, without passing unfriendly people.

21 GET HER TO THE ROOM

Find out each object's weight in relation to each other. Four cutlery sets = two silver bowls, so two cutlery sets = one silver bowl. If four silver bowls = two candelabras, then eight cutlery sets = two candelabras and four cutlery sets = one candelabra. Six cutlery sets = two vases, therefore three cutlery sets = one vase. Therefore, one vase and three silver bowls = nine cutlery sets, and as one candelabra = four cutlery sets, you will need five more cutlery sets to balance out the bags.

22 FIND HIS FILE

Petherbridge's card is the seven of spades, and his file number is D7. The number of his card and the file are the same, but Myron's card is a face card. Notice that there are ten files in the drawers on the left, and three on the right. This indicates that number cards come from the left-hand drawers, and face cards from the right. There are four rows of drawers and four suits. As Spades are in drawer D and the note says to remember alphabetical order, it makes sense that Hearts, which is third alphabetically, would be drawers C and G. So Myron's King of Hearts card indicates his file is G13.

23 OPEN THE BOX

The box needs four dominoes to be inserted into its lid. The dominos each have two numbers on them. Their order is indicated by the shields that represent the four sons: Arvid the One-Toothed, Magnus Single-Fang, Erik the Half-Sighted and Ragnar Lone-Eye. Work out which shield is which son, and then which region each son ruled. Two of the shields, C and D, can be flipped over. However, A and B cannot, so the one-toothed A must be either Arvid or Magnus, and the one-eyed B must be either Erik or Ragnar. According to the saga, Erik lost his right eye (left from our perspective) so B must be Ragnar. Erik must be either D or C flipped. Magnus lost all but his left tooth (right from our perspective) so Magnus must be C, as A and D flipped both have only a right tooth. Therefore Arvid is A and Erik is D.

The story says that all the brothers were happy; Arvid claimed the West and Erik claimed the South. Magnus didn't want the East, so he must have got the North, leaving Ragnar the East.

A Arvid the One-Toothed (west)
B Ragnar Lone-Eye (east)
C Magnus Single-Fang (north)
D Erik the Half-Sighted (south)

1 = |

2 = ↲

3 = ⼂

4 = ≶

5 = ⋔

6 = ⊟

The runes have as many lines as the number they represent.

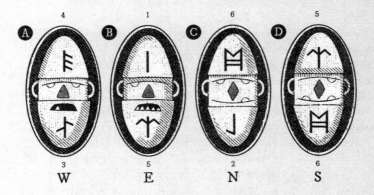

On the box's surface are four directional arrows, showing the order the sons must come: South, West, East, North. So the dominoes should be placed on the lid of the box as follows:

24 SOLVE THE MYSTERY

The myroglyphics key gives the letters A=F, which are also present on the four memorandum lists. If you look at the faces you can see their eyes are either looking up, down, left or right. This indicates from which list you must take the word. The code is: →D, ↑A, ↑E, ↓C, ←C, ↑A, ↑F, ↓C. These words combine to make the phrase:

| FOLLOW | THE | LARGE | BOOKS |
| IGNORE | THE | SMALL | BOOKS |

Follow the lines on the large books and ignore all the others, and you will find a consistent path. Begin with the large book with lines like the base of an arrow. The path ends with the book you must pull.

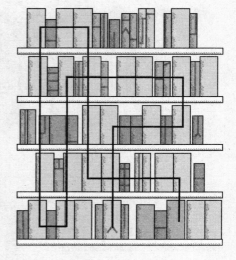

25 DISGUISE YOURSELF

The five items you seek are all depicted in his painting, which matches up with the cabin's floorplan. However, while the the artist's name is Arthur Tisdale, the picture is signed TA, so the painting in fact mirrors the floorplan. So each item's position is in fact on the opposite of where the painting shows them to be, best found by holding the page up to the light. Now you know their general position, you can use the diary and Parrot instructions to work out where they are.

The glasses are behind the key to Paris. (Tisdale said that they represent Freedom, like keys, which are used to unlock things.)

The straw hat is in the drawer underneath the Paris poster. (Tisdale said the hat represented France to him.)

The bow tie is tied around the hourglass. (They have a similar shape.)

The jacket is actually hung on the parrot cage. (The real cover is on the floor, looking like a rug. To Tisdale, jackets represent confinement, or cages.)

The beard is on the portrait of Tisdale's father. (He says his father would disapprove of where it was, as well as indicating he associated the two.)

26 FIND THE ERRORS

Poseidon: A) His trident is an impossible fork; B) There is a food can on the ground which did not exist in 620 BC; C) The ship also did not exist at this time.

Poseidon 620 BC

Knight: A) He is holding a butter knife instead of a halberd; B) He has three hands; C) He's wearing modern boots.

Vitruvian Man: A) He is holding a spoon; B) He lacks the extra two arms and legs; C) He has a fig leaf protecting his modesty.

Britannia: A) Her spear is a paintbrush; B) Her shield is a dinner plate; C) She has a cat behind her.

The common element all four drawings have is a piece of dinnerware, so the rendezvous is at the À la Carte Restaurant.

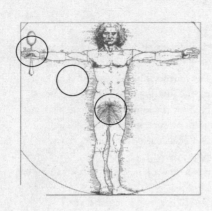

27 DECODE THE MESSAGE

The numbers on the note are all odd (except for the 2) and only divisible by themselves and one, which makes them all prime numbers, as indicated by the key. The grid shows that X = 89. Extrapolate the following code key: A = 2; B = 3; C = 5; D = 7; E = 11; F = 13; G = 17; H = 19; I = 23; J = 29; K = 31; L = 37; M = 41; N = 43; O = 47; P = 53; Q = 59; R = 61; S = 67; T = 71; U = 73; V = 79; W = 83; X = 89; Y = 97; The note on the key with the Z crossed out indicates that Z should not be included. Using that key, the message spells out: THE KEY THAT OPENS THE BAG IS IN THE CROW'S NEST.

28 DEFEAT SHARP

To form a correct chain of moves, you need to insure that at the end of each move you are in position for another move. For example, vaulting the railing in the first bout leaves you hanging over the railing, and none of the following moves begin in that position. The correct chain is: A) Defensive crouch (standing to crouching); C) Disarm (crouching to standing with arms outstretched); B) Block (standing with arms outstretched to standing with arms crossed against face). C) Coup de grâce (standing to victory)!

29 FIND THE ANSWER

Follow the poem's directions and draw lines between the points it references. One line runs from Glory's empty hand to Honour's stylus, to the point where their gazes meet and ending at 7 o'clock. The other line runs from the centre of the wreath to the centre of the world, to Honour's knee, to Glory's empty hand, to the point their gazes meet and ending on Honour's stylus.

Therefore, the number is 42. The poem indicates that clock's hands should be at 4 and 2 and the line 'It's easy as pie to see' suggests you should find the pie that has the same shape as the clock's hands: the scallop pie. The 'number of the clock is in their quantity', so count the scallops on the clock, which gives its number: number seven.

30 CHANGE THE TIME

Follow the circuit symbols to find this path on the diagram:

If you trace the same path on the 5 x 5 grid of clocks, you will pass a clock twenty-two times, as follows:

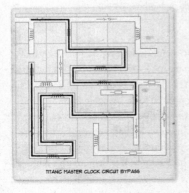

TITANIC MASTER CLOCK CIRCUIT BYPASS

The hexagonal grid is marked 'Hour then Minute'. This indicates that, beginning from the 'start' point, you draw lines following first the hour hand, then the minute hand, of each of the twenty-two clocks.

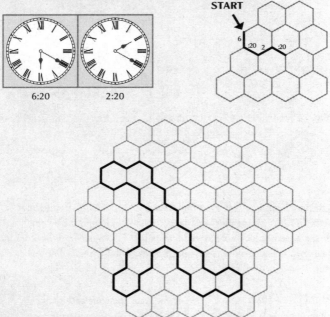

6:20   2:20

This shows that the required metal plate is λ or lambda.

31 GET THE INSTRUMENTS

The piano would travel 55 feet in 1 minute 50 seconds, just over half the length of the corridor. If the tie is on the left, then that means Jock's cabin is B29. If Jock had to turn right to get to it, the violinist's cabin must be B22, B24, B26, or B28 across the corridor. If the double bass player is next door to Jock, his cabin must be B27 or B31. With three rooms separating the bassist and the cellist, the cellist can only be in B35 or B23. The violinist used to be in the upper half of the corridor opposite the double bass player, so the bassist must be in cabin B31. This means the cellist is in cabin B23 and the violinist in in B22, which shares a wall with William's cabin which has the piano.

ESCAPE THE TITANIC

32 COUNT THE BULLETS

Count all the times the gun has been fired, including the times in the previous challenges. In Challenge 30 the steward fired the gun once into the air and said that he had five shots left. In Challenge 30 he fired the gun into the air again. In Challenge 32, you see two bullet holes in the picture of J.P. Morgan, a bullet hole in the porthole window and, if you look at the wallpaper's pattern you will see a circle where there should be a square, indicating it is in fact a bullet hole.

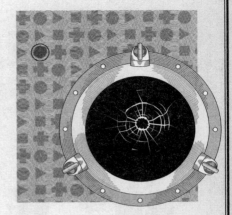

The steward has no bullets left in his gun.

33 SEND A MESSAGE

The translucent cloth forms shapes similar to semaphore flags, but they don't match existing positions, unless, as the men indicated, you turn your head to the left by 45 degrees. Once you do that, you will see that the design of the squares matches the following semaphore positions:

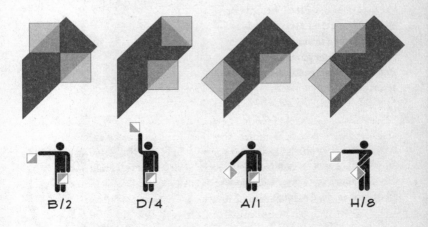

The last four numbers are 2418.

34 OUTSMART SHARP

The correct answers to the questions are:
1) B. There was no diving board; 2) B. Their surnames are the wrong way round;
3) C. The Hello George is not the second fastest (it's actually the slowest); 4) C.
Dionea muscipula is not a healing plant. 5) B. If you combine the shapes of Key A
and Key B you get the shape of Key D: Therefore, if you combine the shapes of Key
C and Key E you also get the shape of Key D.

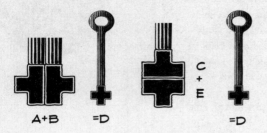

35 OPEN THE WATCH

First you have to work out which
direction to turn the globe, and by
how much. Alexander told Linneaus
'the departure and arrival should be on
his hands', and the Latin inscriptions
read 'Depart on the minute. Arrive on
the hour. Turn the globe 45 degrees
anticlockwise, the hands will point at the
departure and arrival points.

If you turn the watch over and turn the
top symbols 45 degrees anticlockwise,
they will match up to show numbers at
each of the cardinal points.

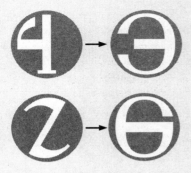

North = 4; South = 3; East = 2; West = 6

The arrows at the centre of the symbols show how these numbers should be connected: North to South, East to West.

When you draw lines between IV and III and between II and VI, they intersect at a point on the globe in Scotland. That is where you must press to open the watch.

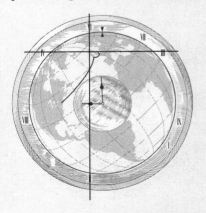

36 ESCAPE THE TITANIC

The equation helps you deduce the value of the symbols, but it's important to notice that the value is defined by certain elements in the pictures.

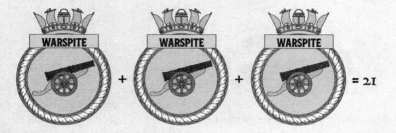

3 x Warspite = 21, so Warspite = 7.

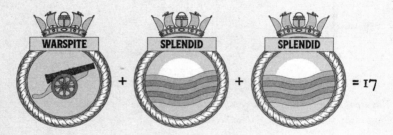

Warspite + Splendid + Splendid is 17, so Splendid must be 10 ÷ 2, or 5. There are five stripes on the Splendid symbol so each stripe on Splendid is worth 1.

Splendid with five stripes (5) + Turbulent x Gleaner (8) = 125. So Turbulent is 15 with 5 stars.

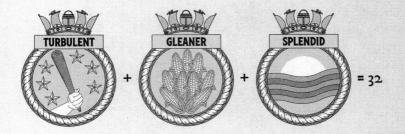

Turbulent with six stars (18) + Gleaner with nine sheafs (9) + Splendid with five stripes (5) = 32. Splendid has 5 stripes, Gleaner has 9 sheafs and Turbulent has 6 stars, so each wheat stalk on Gleaner is worth 1 and each star on Turbulent is worth 3. So the symbols indicate the following boats: A is 8; B is 7; C is 15; D is 12; E is 9; F is 6; G is 18; H is 5. Lifeboat 18 is indicated by symbol G.

Notes

Notes

Picture credits